HARVEY PUBLIC LIBRARY DISTRICT
W9-AWA-313

Reproduction Is the Flaw of Love

Reproduction Is the Flaw of Love

Lauren Grodstein

THE DIAL PRESS

REPRODUCTION IS THE FLAW OF LOVE
A Dial Press Book / July 2004

Published by
The Dial Press
A Division of Random House, Inc.
New York, New York

Book design by Ox and Company

Library of Congress Cataloging-in-Publication Data
Grodstein, Lauren.
Reproduction is the flaw of love : a novel / Lauren Grodstein.
p. cm.
ISBN 0-385-33770-1
1. Bachelors—Fiction. 2. Young men—Fiction. 3. New York (N.Y.)—Fiction.
4. Man-woman relationships—Fiction. 5. Pregnancy—Signs and diagnosis—Fiction.
I. Title.
PS3607.R63R46 2004
813'.6—dc22 2003070001

Manufactured in the United States of America
Published simultaneously in Canada

10 9 8 7 6 5 4 3 2 1
BVG

for Ben

PART ONE

(Primarily Concerning a Baby)

Five Minutes Ago

Miller wanted to go to Rite Aid, but Lisa wanted him to go to Smith Drug, and this is what they found themselves fighting about in the sticky five minutes after she announced that her period was late. "It's probably nothing," she said. "Go to Smith and grab me an E.P.T. stick. And also some more Crest. We're almost out."

"There's a new tube under the sink," Miller told her. "What do you mean, it's probably nothing? How late are you?"

Lisa sighed and stuck a pen in between the pages of the book she was reading, to hold her place. This was how she liked to fight: sighing and feigning distraction. The book was *Mrs. Bridge*. "Six days. And there's no new tube under the sink—that's the one we just finished. Go to Smith Drug," she repeated.

"Rite Aid's closer."

"Smith's independent."

"It's raining out."

"I thought we were going to support the little guys."

"You might be pregnant."

"Miller," she said to him, and picked her book back up. "It's probably nothing."

He looked at her face closely, to see if she meant it—was it Nothing? or maybe this was really Something?—but she closed her eyes and yawned and it was impossible to determine. This felt strange to him, because Lisa was rarely impossible.

Miller rolled his eyes at the dog. The dog snuffled and yawned. This all happened five minutes ago.

Some Background

Joel Miller and Lisa Stanislaw live together in Brooklyn, in three small rooms painted yellow. The apartment belonged to Lisa before Miller moved in, and therefore Miller suffers certain daily indignities—lacy ruffled curtains, a teakettle shaped like a duck, a black-and-white poster, over the television, of a towheaded boy offering flowers to a towheaded girl. When Miller moved in eight months ago, he and Lisa made compromises—he was allowed to smoke indoors; she was allowed to keep that fucking poster. So.

These days, despite their respective concessions, the pair make admirable roommates, agreeing on grocery store decisions and bathroom cleaning and music. They gladly pay for air-conditioning, but have jointly vetoed cable. They play the Stones and Chaka Khan on the CD player. They like to cook ravioli together, and three to four times a week enjoy brisk, healthy sex. They also share the yawning, snuffling dog, Harry, and, to sum up, rarely step on each other's toes. It is a peaceable existence.

The corner of Brooklyn that Lisa and Miller inhabit is called Park Slope: leafy blocks jammed with renovated brownstones and cheery ice-cream parlors and taped-up flyers announcing lost cats or stoop sales. Lisa has lived here for six years—since three days after her Barnard graduation—and Miller knows that she prides herself on being very much of the neighborhood. Storekeepers wave to her on her walk home; she smiles and waves back. Her favorite mornings are the ones in bright summer when Long Island farmers set up stalls at the mouth of Prospect Park and call it a "greenmarket." On these mornings,

Lisa wakes up early to jostle for dented blueberries and slightly viscous zucchini bread. As for Miller, it took him a while to acclimate to the Park Slope penchants for eating organic and supporting independent businesses. Before Brooklyn, he'd lived on the Upper East Side and drank two Starbucks mocha lattes daily. Although the lattes made Miller feel girly, their Starbucks provenance never left him feeling like a bad citizen.

But his girl has her ideas.

Lisa is, currently, a first-grade teacher with a broken leg. Miller finds her pretty in a quiet way: long brown hair, straight nose, small chin. She wears straw hats and ankle-length batik skirts. Once in a while Miller wishes she'd get a nose ring, dye her hair platinum, or tattoo a flower on her ankle. He wishes she'd come home in a black leather miniskirt, and occasionally it fills him with a sad resignation to know she never will.

Nevertheless, Miller is quite attached to each of Lisa's charms: clear skin, generous spirit, big breasts, conscientious nature. She is an optimist, and comes equipped with an abiding love of the underdog; hence Prospect Park over Central, the bus over the subway, the *Atlantic Monthly* over the *New Yorker*. She's forever handing out change to panhandlers and smiling at babies in strollers. She organizes an annual winter coat drive at the school where she teaches. She pays her bills on time.

"I think it's still raining," Miller says.

"It should be clearing any moment." Another thing about Lisa: she always knows the forecast.

And yet, while Miller is grateful for all the good things about his girl, he finds it troubling that, taken as a whole, they are usually no challenge to the memory of the girl who came before her.

• • •

Harry the dog noses around Lisa's cast, which is starting to smell a bit funky after two weeks bound to her leg during a sticky, humid spring. "Oh, Harry-bones," Lisa says, tickling him under his hairy gray chin. She loves Harry, spoils him, treats him to whole roasted marrow bones she orders off the Internet. "You'd go to the pharmacy for me, wouldn't you? You'd do a favor for a poor girl with a broken leg, right?"

"For God's sake." Miller glowers. How he wishes that Lisa had gone on the pill like a normal woman. Each of his previous girlfriends had been on the pill, and as far as Miller knows, not a single one of them had ever gotten pregnant. But, no, Lisa can't stand birth control pills; they make her feel bloated, moody, aggressive, sleepy, angry, sad. They are an unnatural intervention in her body's biorhythms. Lisa prefers condoms.

"You know, maybe if you had stayed on the pill . . ." he says.

"Miller," she groans, withdrawing her hand from Harry's chin. "Please go."

The rain outside their front-room windows beats down loudly. "Smith is twelve blocks away," he says.

"Why are you being a pain about this?"

"I'm just saying . . ." he protests. "It's raining out, and who knows if Smith even sells E.P.T.?"

"Smith sells E.P.T.," she says. "And if they don't, get me a different test. I don't care. Do you need money?"

"I have money," he says. "It's not about money."

"Miller, I really want to get this test taken care of. Today. Like now. We've got Bonnie's dinner thing tonight and I won't be able to eat otherwise."

"Do you really think you're pregnant?"

"I don't know," she says. She sighs again and leans her head back against the cushions of the greenish plaid sofa they found together at a garage sale. She is wearing one of his old T-shirts and a pair of her own shorts, her cast propped up on the chipped glass coffee table. It is eleven A.M. on a cool gray Saturday. It is April. There is no way, Miller thinks, that she can be pregnant.

"Listen," she says. "Don't worry. If it turns out I am, we'll figure something out." She pulls her hair off her face, and he can see the knotty veins through the skin of her hands. He can also see that her hands are trembling.

"Of course we will," Miller says, hit with an unexpected whoosh of sympathy. "We'll figure it out." He sits down next to her and kisses her. He puts a hand on her cool right cheek. "You're not pregnant, you know."

"But I might be."

He kisses her again. "I'll be back soon."

She nods, smiles primly, and turns back to her book. And so Miller walks the twelve blocks to Smith Drug soaking wet, because despite Lisa's forecasting it's still raining, and Miller didn't want to ask her where to find the umbrella.

In the Life of Joel J. Miller, Some Close Calls So Far:

1. The very first time he stole anything. During one November lunch hour in the first grade, Miller pilfered seventy-four cents from the money jar Mrs. DeCesare kept on the far left corner of her desk. Young Miller had wanted the seventy-four cents to buy a Chocolate Dream Bar at the fifth-grade ice-cream sale; even though Chocolate Dreams only cost sixty cents, he figured he might as well take what he could. He closed the jar just as DeCesare reentered the room, and when she saw him alone in the darkened classroom, she seemed to grow worried and then quickly annoyed. "Go to the fifth-grade ice-cream sale," she commanded, in a voice paved with nicotine and irritation. He followed her instructions, clutching the contraband nickels and pennies in his sweaty little palm. If DeCesare ever noticed that the money jar was short seventy-four cents, she never pinned the larceny on him. He got lucky. Nevertheless, for months following the incident, Miller suffered from guilty nightmares, and knew fear.

2. The Friday night that Allie Friedman first gave him a blow job on her parents' bed. Allie was his twelfth-grade girlfriend, and in defense of them both, the blow job episode was not as sordid as one might initially assume. In fact, Allie was using the oral ministrations to maintain her virginity for as long as she could. Miller, a jaded seventeen, sorely longed for more. He had tried all the standard horny-adolescent stratagems: the testaments to eternal devotion, the appeal to reason ("it's gotta go sometime"), and the declaration that he knew she couldn't enjoy giving head as much as she swore up and down that she did. Dear Allie. One night a few months later, after Miller had finally wrestled her to the floor in an extended make-out session, messed around under her hot, damp panties for a good twenty minutes, told her that he loved her, and made his standard appeal to reason, she exhaled and said, "Jesus, fine, I can't *take* it anymore." But the look in her eyes was one of such profound resignation that he immediately lost his hard-on and ended up remaining a virgin until his freshman year at Brown. As for the close call: Allie was tending to Miller on her parents' bed (they liked it in there, because they could watch racy movies on HBO while they dry-humped), when Mr. and Mrs. Friedman got home from the theater an hour before their estimated time of arrival. Allie, sweet, cautious Allie, heard the garage door opening, zipped Miller up, and wiped her lips just as the front door closed; Mr. and Mrs. Friedman found them, improbably, sitting in the hallway between Allie's bedroom and their own, "just talking," Miller hunched over and legs crossed to hide his pulsing erection, Allie leaning drowsily against a wall. He was sure he could hear both their hearts pounding through their shirts. However, much like good Mrs. DeCesare,

if the Friedmans thought anything strange about the scene they happened in on, neither of them ever said a word.

3. The time that Miller found Harry, the dog. Some kind of moronic sheepdog half-breed. Goofy, loyal, overweight Harry, who once upon a time was a mangy and bedraggled collection of fur and bones, living in an ASPCA cage that afforded him approximately four inches of space on either side. He'd been slowly dying there for weeks. Miller had wandered into the ASPCA in order to impress Blair Carter, who thought he needed a pet in his life—and Miller wanted to prove to her that he could take care of things besides himself. Truthfully, he had no intention of actually adopting a pet, but he thought that walking himself into the ASPCA offices was at least a nod to the right intentions. Barbara, the kindly dwarf who was working the adoption desk that particular Friday, took one look at Miller and said, "I've got the dog for you." She ignored him when he protested that he was really in the market for a cat, maybe, or a parakeet. "I don't have time for a dog," Miller said. "I don't even *like* dogs particularly." But when she brought him to Harry's cage, and the dog looked at Miller with the saddest canine eyes in the world, he knew that Barbara was right. Harry came home and pissed all over the rug in the glee of liberation, but Blair simply cleaned it up and kissed Miller hard and told him that he had done something valiant. He wasn't sure about that, but he was pleased to have pleased the girl. And glad that he'd gotten to Harry just in the nick.
4. The time Miller told Blair Carter that he loved her. They were at a party. The music was loud. They stood in the kitchen. "What?" she said. "It's noisy in here." "I love you," Miller repeated. "What?" she said. He

> thought for a second, and then said, "Oh. Just—nothing." He picked up some bottles of tonic. They went back in to the loud music, the vodka, and their friends. While the rest of the party went off without further incident, Miller spent hours afterward thinking about what might have happened had she heard and chosen to respond. What would she have said?

When recounting these events to himself, Miller often considers that four out of four of his close calls have been precipitated by women. He assumes that most men would say the same about their own trickiest bits of history.

And now he's standing in aisle three at Smith Drug, because that's where Lisa told him to go. Once again, he's doing what the lady told him to do. Miller's the only customer in the store, scanning the dusty collection of pregnancy tests—certainly no E.P.T. stick; all the boxes look like they predate Ms. magazine—and he's dripping a puddle onto the linoleum floor. The pharmacist (Smith, he assumes) is staring at him coldly from behind his wood-veneer perch at the back of the store, pens poking from the pocket of his thin cotton shirt, gray hairs pasted over the dome of his head. His expression gives Miller the willies. This is what you get for supporting the independent businessman, Miller thinks.

He picks up a box called CleanTest Pink and reads the instructions, which involve urine, two cups, and one tab. He thinks to himself that tests like these are probably best left to a laboratory. Miller himself has never liked chemistry. "Is this all you have?" he calls out to Smith.

Smith continues scowling. "What else you want?" he asks.

"You have the thing with the—the thing with the stick?"

"We got what we got," he says, with the pithiness of a man who believes sympathy is for losers. Miller nods at him, picks up the CleanTest Pink, and grabs a tube of Crest from the front of the aisle. The Crest, too, looks ancient—the typeface on the box has a decidedly nineteen-eighties slant. Oh, well. The woman at the register, short and wizened (Mrs. Smith?), asks Miller for entirely too much money for his two items. Because he has other things to worry about, he doesn't complain.

Back Home

And so here it is. A rainy April day, a Saturday, a day that began with too-strong coffee and a Camel Light on the front stoop. Over his cigarette, Miller had considered some Saturday plans: a walk to the Community Bookstore, perhaps, and a stop at the dry cleaner's to pick up Lisa's school clothes. Get some bagels at Terrace Bagels, finish reading *The Master and Margarita*. See if Lisa wanted to rent a movie, maybe play Scrabble—entertainment that would keep her immobile in respect to her leg. Buy some wine to bring to Bonnie's. As he smoked and deliberated, the sky turned gray and it began to rain.

He thinks to himself now, as he approaches that same stoop, that maybe he should be cataloging the events of the day for future retellings. If today is the day that Miller finds out he's going to be a father, then surely there's a certain momentousness to its events, however outwardly mundane. Even his little jaunt to the drugstore this morning might find its way into an anecdote that will embarrass, in the future, his future son. He's glad he went to Smith's, then. Rite Aid is so sterile.

If he's going to be a father in the first place.

If that's what he's going to be.

It's only as he approaches the stoop that the thought of a child hits Miller with something like urgency—not when Lisa told him that her period was late, not when he bought the CleanTest Pink, not even when Mrs. Smith smiled at him on his way out and wished him, unexpectedly, good luck. He might be a father. Everything is unfamiliar.

A little green ball, a child's ball, bounces across the street and lands on Miller's front stoop. Fuck, he thinks to himself. Not what he had planned on. Although somewhere inside him a voice yells:

Children, of course, yes! Little Millers with freckles and moppy brown hair and brown eyes and scabby knees! Millers who play baseball and soccer, who get good grades, who get blow jobs on their parents'—on his!—bed! Yes! Millers who have mothers named Lisa! Report cards! Minivans!

But wait. Miller has never been to India or Thailand or Russia. He has always wanted to go. He's never even been to Las Vegas. Never played shortstop for a Major League Baseball team. Or minor. Never went dune-skiing in the Sahara. Never slept with a woman who doesn't speak English. And now, he knows—let's face it, he knows—that he never will. Miller will be twenty-nine next month.

A child, a little girl in a raincoat—maybe four? five?—runs up to the stoop, grabs the ball, and clutches it to her chest with both arms. She gives Miller a nasty look before she darts back across the street. What hateful creatures children are. What tyrants!

The rain is clearing, so Miller sits down on the stoop and shakes out a Camel. He wishes he'd known beforehand how much he disliked children. Maybe, he thinks, he would have thought twice before relying on condoms to stick it to Lisa.

• • •

She's already in the bathroom when Miller walks into the apartment. Her crutches are inside with her. He tries to open the bathroom door, but it's locked.

"Why are you already in the bathroom?"

"Getting ready," she says through the door. "Mental preparation. Did you get the test?"

"Yeah," he says. "Well, sort of."

"Sort of?" She opens the door a crack and Miller hands her

the CleanTest Pink; she closes the door again. From where he stands, he can hear the package being torn open and then a groan. "You need a doctorate to figure this out!"

"Do you want me to come in and help?"

"No," she says. "I'll do this by myself."

"You sure?" In general, Miller likes to leave Lisa alone in the bathroom, but he knows that today other rules apply.

"Sure I'm sure," Lisa says. There's a pause, and he can hear her unfolding paper.

"Do you think we should have a talk first?" He probably should have asked her this already.

"What do you want to talk about?"

He tries the sooty crystal knob on the bathroom door. She's locked it again. "The results."

"We don't know what the results are yet."

"Possible results," he says. "Potential."

"Nothing to talk about until we know what's what," she says. Through the door he can hear more paper ruffle. "This is the best pregnancy test they had?"

He pinches his knuckle to keep from reminding her that Smith Drug was *her* idea. "Yes," he says. "I'm going to smoke a cigarette, honey," he adds.

"Fine," she says. "I think I figured this out anyway. The first step is just to pee in the cup."

"Great," he says. "Good. You can do that. Pee in the cup."

He hears the cool porcelain clink when she flips up the toilet lid.

"Okay," he says. "I'll be right here." Miller sits down on the floor near the bathroom, lights another cigarette, and waits for Lisa to pee.

Something Miller's Father Once Said

Here is something that Miller's father once said to him, on a cloudy summer morning a few weeks after Miller had turned fourteen: "Don't do the deed, son, if you don't want to face the consequences."

"What?" Miller had asked. He'd been playing with a scab he'd picked off his knee and weighing whether or not to eat it.

"The deed, son," Stanley B. Miller said. "There will be consequences. Always are."

Miller shrugged and crunched the scab between his fingers. "You talking about something in particular, dad?"

"I'm talking about . . . son, you know what I'm talking about." Miller shrugged again. It was true. The fourteen-year-old Miller did know what his father was talking about, but because they both referred to that "it" elliptically, he liked to clarify with his father that the subject he suspected they were talking about was, indeed, the subject they *were* talking about before he committed himself to a response.

"So?" Miller asked.

"I just want to make sure you know what you're getting yourself into."

Miller put his finger on his knee, to stop the blood from welling underneath where the scab had been. He knew what he was getting himself into. His parents were getting divorced, and he had decided to live with his mother, Bay, rather than with Stan, despite the myriad complications that were sure to arise from this decision. Stan was not so much disappointed as he was concerned.

"I know what I'm doing," Miller said.

"Of course, son, of course."

"I've been paying attention."

Miller's mother had been losing her tether to happiness for years, in much the same way that a slippery-fingered child lets go of a balloon. Dr. Weintraub, Bay's shrink, kept changing her prescriptions along with his diagnosis: first it was chronic fatigue, then severe anxiety disorder, then mania, then depression. What all this generally meant was that during the past three years his mother had become more tired, angry, and sad.

"Stay here or come with me, kid," Stan said. "Either way, there will be consequences."

Miller didn't think he was on to anything in particular. They were sitting along the creek that ran through the backyard of the family's New Jersey half-acre. Miller was throwing pebbles at tadpoles. "What would you do if you were me?" he asked his father, as another tadpole darted away.

"Hard to know," Stan said. He sat down next to Miller in his slow, overweight way, crouching down to a squat. He was wearing tan shorts and his knees looked as big as coconuts. Miller sometimes felt that if his father didn't leave soon, he could die. He was breathing heavily through his mouth, as had become his habit.

"All my stuff is here," Miller said.

"Not such a big deal," Stan said. He lowered himself farther, until he was sitting flat on his ass next to his son. Miller knew that his mother was watching them from the kitchen window, smoking, pulling at her knotty brown hair. "The movers will take it with us."

Miller shrugged.

"Or we could just get you new stuff," Stan said. "What do you want, a new stereo?" he asked. "A new record player?"

Miller shrugged again.

"It's hard, moving," Stan said. "People are resistant to change." He picked up a pebble and jiggled it around in his hand. "I'm a little nervous myself, son, if you want the truth."

Miller looked up at his father's wide face, and at his scalp, the color of salmon. He knew that Stan had stuck around for as long as he did out of a drifty sense of guilt, but Bay's constant weeping and hectoring were becoming more than even a generally phlegmatic man like his father could stand. Stan's business trips were growing longer, and he was taking more of them. When he came home from the office he often went straight to bed. And now, finally, since puberty seemed around the corner for Miller, his father had decided to make a run for it. He didn't need to feel guilty. Miller would be an adult soon enough, and could make his own choices.

"Listen," Stan added, "she'll be okay, if that's what you're worried about."

"She's fragile."

"Sure she is," Stan said. "But she knows how to take care of herself. And we'll only be twenty minutes away." He kept jiggling the pebble. "By car."

"I can't drive," Miller said.

"I'll teach you."

"Dad," Miller said, "I'm fourteen." He threw his pebbles across the creek at the maple tree on the other side. Six or seven years before, while Stan was away on business, Miller and his mother had nailed slats up the trunk of that maple to make a ladder. They'd sat up top in the branches and eaten peanut butter sandwiches for dinner. The slats still hung there, though the nails were rusty.

"I think I better stay," Miller said, after a few more pebbles had bounced off the tree. "I don't think it's a good idea for us both to leave."

"Ah," Stan sighed. He clapped Miller on the shoulder, twice, hard. Miller thought that maybe he could see relief in his father's expression.

When Stan moved out the following Saturday, he took as little as possible. A suitcase, some old records, a few files. His treasured baseball card collection, carried in a series of leatherette cases. At last count, Stan had more than thirteen hundred baseball cards—one hundred and eighty Hall of Famers.

Miller and his mother sat on the front step and watched.

"Don't forget your socks, Stan," she said each time he went into the house. "I don't want to see your goddamn socks in my goddamn laundry anymore."

Miller's father continued to load the car in silence: a small brown duffel, a collection of maps, his old *Field Guide to Prescription Pharmaceuticals*, two saucepans and a pot.

"Your socks, Stan," his mother muttered. She kept lighting new cigarettes and stubbing out old ones on the brick step. Miller sat quietly next to her. He wanted to help his dad move his stuff, but he didn't want to upset his mother.

When it was finally time for Stan to get into the Cadillac and drive the twenty minutes to Fort Lee, Miller allowed himself to be swept up in his big, crushing arms. "Take care of your mom, son," he said. Then, like he was reading lines from a screenplay, Stan told Miller that he was a good kid. Miller could feel Stan's heart racing. After a minute or two, Stan let go, and Miller buckled back down on the steps. Bay stood.

"You'll come visit?" she asked.

"I'll be around tomorrow," he said. "Or the day after."

She nodded, then wiped a tear from under her eye. "I'm so sorry, Stan," she said, and she wrapped her arms around his neck and kissed him, standing there, clinging to him in a soap-opera kiss, a movie-star kiss. Miller had never seen his parents do anything like that before. He picked up one of his mother's still-burning cigarette stubs and mashed it into the step.

Stan whispered something to Bay, and kissed her again. Then he picked up his last suitcase, patted Miller on the head, and drove off. Miller and his mother watched him go. After a while, Bay went back inside to make sure Stan hadn't left any socks. Miller stayed there, on the steps, as still as he could possibly be, for as long as he possibly could.

Three Kinds of Men Miller Promised His Mother He Wouldn't Become:

1. A Man Who Lies to His Woman
2. A Man Who Lies to His Mother
3. A Man Who Leaves

So far, in his almost twenty-nine years of existence, Miller has made a fair attempt to keep these promises to his mother. Frequently he has failed. Of course he failed! He has done his share of lying to the various women in his life, and he has done more than his share of lying to his mother. However, when he recounts these episodes in his head, he tends to rely on a dodgy self-defense: that these lies have often—or perhaps always—been for their recipients' own good. It is quite rare, he believes, that he lies to get himself out of trouble.

The third promise has been easier for Miller to keep than the first two, however. He does not leave. He never has. He stayed with his mother in that dusty, ashy house in New Jersey until she sold it. When he moved up to Providence to go to school, Bay moved to San Francisco to be close to her sister. As far as Miller was concerned, she was leaving him as much as he was leaving her. And as for the other women in his life—well, Allie Friedman and he came to their mutual end after a series of disagreements concerning her virginity; the split was concordantly agreed upon and amicable. In college, Julia Lopez taught him to appreciate classical music—Stravinsky, Mozart—and then left for Juilliard to study it. After college, Debra Fox left for Los Angeles to star in commercials. And then Blair Carter—Blair just left. Miller still wonders, sometimes, if she'll come back.

All of which goes to show, he thinks, that he's the type who sticks around. He's a stand-up guy. And if, he reasons, Lisa places three drops of urine into a cup, swirls it around, sticks a tab in it, and provides them both with a little bit of not-so-surprising-anymore news, then Miller will do what it is he has to do. Which is to say, he'll stay right here. He's almost sure he won't go anywhere else.

Your Neutered Pet and You

Miller has smoked his cigarette to the filter, so he drops it into an empty Diet Coke can and calls to Lisa through the bathroom door. "How's it going in there?"

"Oh, you know," she says. "Everything's fine."

"You sure?"

"Maybe," she says, "maybe it would help if you got me a beverage."

"Orange juice?" he asks. "Beer?"

"Water," she says. "Or actually a beer would be good."

"Hey," he says. "Not if you're pregnant."

She's silent in there for a second, then says, "Oh. Right."

Miller walks to the kitchen and fishes a bottle of Poland Spring from the refrigerator. With unusual care, he wipes clean a glass from the drying rack, fills it halfway with ice, and pours the water in. He brings both the glass and the bottle to the bathroom door.

"Your beverage, my dear," he says. She opens the door a crack, leaning on her crutches, her broken leg trailing stiffly behind her on the floor like a tent pole.

"Thanks," she says, and, closing an armpit over each crutch, she drinks the entire glass of water at once. She grimaces, as though it were sour medicine.

"A little stopped up, huh?" he asks.

Her eyes are closed. Miller notices that she's wearing sparkly silver eye shadow, and her lips have been painted bright red. She smiles, abashed.

He kisses her on her red mouth and feels her lipstick smear against his lips. It's arousing. He pulls her in carefully, so as not to disturb her equilibrium. "You can do it," he whispers in her ear. "Don't worry."

"Right," she says. She wipes the lipstick off his face. "Of course I can do it. Pee in a cup. Please." She nods at Miller; they are in agreement about her capabilities. "So leave," she says. "Let me try again."

"You're sure? I could stay."

"Nope," she says. "Unnecessary. Go away. I want a little privacy."

Miller closes the bathroom door and leans against it. He takes a long look at their fastidious apartment, sees a playpen near his CD collection, a box of diapers on the bookshelf. He makes eye contact with his languorous dog, who galumphs over with the leash in his mouth.

"C'mon, man, it's gross outside," Miller tells him. "And Lisa might be pregnant." But now the dog hustles to the front door and scratches at the wood. His ass jiggles like an old lady's.

"It's fine, Miller," Lisa calls through from the other side of the bathroom door. "Take him out. I need a little quiet in here anyway."

"I'm not giving you quiet?" he asks, wounded.

"You know," she says. "I mean, I just want a little . . . Just take him out. If you don't mind."

"Okay," Miller says. "I'll be back in five." He looks out their front window; the rain seems to be holding, and this might be the only chance he has for the rest of the day to get outside alone. Miller puts on a red fleece vest and straightens his glasses. "I'm outta here," he says. He picks up Harry's leash, and the dog dances with enthusiasm.

Harry and Miller walk toward the park slowly, the dog stopping periodically to sniff, and Miller to tie his shoes, to take off his vest, to just stand still. The park is three blocks away and frequently Harry and Miller run there—or, more accurately, Harry runs and Miller gets pulled along, dragged like a can tied to a wedding-day car. But today they are both contemplative. Miller wonders if dogs can predict pregnancy like earthquakes: maybe Lisa's giving off some pheromones that the dog can instinctively acknowledge in its prune-size brain. He wonders if Harry knows the complexities of imminent fatherhood. He imagines not. The dog was neutered years ago. According to the dwarf Barbara at the ASPCA, early neutering was one of the dog's best selling points.

"No pissing on your rugs," she had lied. She was wearing an

ASPCA cap and a child-size Izod shirt and came up to Miller's hip. "No humping your leg."

"Dogs never really want to hump my legs," Miller said. He stared at Barbara, her shrunken shoulders, her smooth, elongated face.

Barbara nodded, sanguine. She seemed like she had made peace with the staring; Miller admired her for that. "Well, still," she said. "Nobody likes a horny mutt."

"I suppose." Miller tore his eyes away from her flat nose, her thick brows, to look at the brochure she handed him. It was called "Your Neutered Pet and You." In the moments before he left the ASPCA with Harry on a leash, he shook Barbara's hand for longer than necessary, delighting in the feel of her childlike fingers and smooth, niblet-size nails. He wondered, later, checking his new pet for visible ticks or fleas, whether or not he was some kind of pervert. He'd heard of such things, men too attached to little women. When Barbara sent him a thank-you note for taking Harry into a new and loving home, Miller saved it.

• • •

Prospect Park, a quadrilateral shot of green in the middle of Brooklyn, was designed by Frederick Law Olmsted, the same man who designed Manhattan's Central Park. But Olmsted considered Prospect, not Central, his masterpiece, and from the particular angle at which he's viewing the place, Miller can understand why. Willow trees bend down into the banks of the central lake, on which swans and ducks glide as if on tracks. Oblivious to the gray skies, joggers pace themselves on the running trails, while mothers push baby carriages on the paved paths near the water. It seems to Miller idyllic in a nineteenth-century way.

An attractive woman with a long blond ponytail walks by with her black Labrador puppy. She is not compelled to stop, but the puppy wants to give Harry his regards; it bounds over and sniffs Harry's ass. Harry responds by licking his own flank furiously, as if embarrassed.

"Sorry," says the woman. "We just brought him home from the breeder. He's getting neutered this week."

"You're kidding," Miller says. "We were just talking about that. Neutering, I mean."

"We?" the woman asks.

"Me and the dog," Miller says. "I have a brochure all about it. In fact, I'm going home now to give it another read."

The woman nods at Miller and yanks at her puppy's leash. "How nice," she says, and hurries toward the lake.

"Neutering is crucial," Miller calls after her. A sharp wind blows against the Prospect Park treetops, shaking leaf-rain into their eyes. "I'll find that brochure when we get back," Miller says as they turn toward home. The dog stops to smell the base of a fire hydrant. "It tells us some things that are important to remember." Harry looks up and wags his tail.

The dog seems, to Miller, to know the facts: animals that have been sterilized are more affectionate than those that have not. They smell better. They live for approximately twice as long and their risk of developing several major cancers is much lower. Perhaps none of this is too surprising. Still, it's hard for Miller not to consider the irony: it is an animal's need to reproduce itself that often makes it so fucking unpleasant in the first place.

Miller can hear his father say it now, stiffly, as if rehearsed. *Remember the consequences, son.* The consequences of indiscriminate fucking. The consequences of discriminate fucking. The consequences of moving in with this broken-legged long-haired grade-school teacher in Park Slope. The consequences of being the guy who sticks around.

Harry's eyes follow the black puppy and his blond owner as they begin to walk along the lake. He seems pensive. Miller scratches his dog on the head as they stand there, near the Fifteenth Street entrance to Prospect Park, considering.

A Stitch in Time

Lisa broke her leg buying tomato sauce. Later, when she was in a kidding mood, Miller told her that this was God's way of punishing her for not making the sauce from scratch. She agreed, and looked balefully at the pile of tomatoes she'd picked up a few days before at the greenmarket. "What was I thinking?" she lamented. "I make a very nice tomato sauce." Then she popped another Tylenol with codeine.

At Lucky's, the bodega down the street from their house, tomato sauce, cans of Progresso soup, jars of mayonnaise, and rolls of paper towels are all kept on the highest shelves. Mr. Wang, the proprietor, has a special hook designed to retrieve any of these smallish roundish items; with a quick swipe and a jaunty bounce, he will catch the exact product you've pointed at and hand it to you with a flourish. But Wang and his hook were busy assisting other customers at the same moment that Lisa set her sights on an oversize jar of San Marzano tomato sauce, and so she decided to try the hook maneuver without Mr. Wang's practiced arm, and without the hook.

As Lisa tells it: She looked around for an appropriate item to assist her in her retrieval and settled on a dense roll of toilet paper from a nearby shelf. She aimed the toilet paper at the bottom of the top jar of sauce, which looked like it was precariously balanced anyway and needed just a little push to bring it down into her arms. Lisa had played softball in high school—she knew her aim to be true and her catch to be good. Moreover, she was in a rush; they were going to Bonnie's for dinner and Lisa had promised to bring a pan of baked ravioli. She had exactly an hour to finish a two-hour job.

She aimed. She threw. She succeeded in hitting the jar at

the exact point she'd hoped, near the bottom, hard enough to dislodge it. The toilet paper boomeranged back, and she caught it in her right hand, all the while waiting for the sauce to finish its slow tip off the top shelf and land in her left. She was feeling, she later admitted, rather proud.

But although Lisa was not a bad science student, she'd never, Miller knew, excelled at grocery store physics, and when the entire five-jar-high pileup collapsed on her, she was surprised, to say the least. She covered her head with her arms; an avalanche of mayonnaise, paper towels, and sauce knocked her to the ground. Miller met her at the hospital. They owed Wang three hundred dollars. Bonnie rescheduled her dinner for two weeks later. Which is tonight. Due to Lisa's current condition, Bonnie told them not to bring anything but themselves.

The last time Lisa and Miller had sex, then, was two weeks ago this morning. Ever since her leg's been broken, she's felt too sweaty, too stiff, too hobbled. Miller has tried telling her that he doesn't care, that she can just lie there if she wants to, that he doesn't think he can wait the eight weeks it'll take for her cast to come off. But then she gives him a look reminiscent of the looks he used to receive from Allie Friedman, and he backs off. He wonders if that's when they conceived: Lisa's last healthy morning two weeks ago. It was a nice morning—Miller can remember it well. They had missionary sex, switched to doggie-style, climaxed; Miller smoked, Lisa went running, and then they met for a tuna-sandwich lunch in the park. Miller came home and caught up on some work. Lisa went to Lucky's. Quite possibly pregnant.

This, too, is something that Miller considers preserving. The Morning His Son Was Conceived. He knows nothing about his own conception, and that's the way he likes it, but he imagines that his mother can remember and that she's glad she knows. And, maybe, he thinks, he'll have a different kind of kid, the kind of kid who understands that his parents are only human. That they indulge in what politicians call "relations" once in a while. Maybe it'll be a tale that his son will tell his own future wife, a funny story for the third or fourth date, when he needs something amusing and personal to share with her, something to make her feel close. "Yup," he'll say. "I was conceived, and then my mother went to the grocery store and broke her fibula. Suffered through three months of morning sickness with a four-pound cast on her leg." And his son's future wife will chuckle at the sitcom-variety hilarity of it all, and the son will smile and shake his head. Miller's boy, all grown up.

Jesus, Miller thinks.

On the way back to the apartment, he and Harry pass the local bakery, an ecumenical establishment that offers Shabbat challahs, Communion pastries, and rococo wedding cakes. On one of their first dates, Lisa and Miller stopped here for a black-and-white cookie, five inches in diameter, and Miller split it carefully so that he and Lisa would each have some black and some white in their respective halves. These days, he buys a shot of bakery espresso each morning on his way to the F train. When he has some extra change in his pocket, he'll add a croissant, a semolina roll, or an early-morning cannoli. "A jump start," he'll explain, even if nobody's listening.

Miller walks into the bakery. He is the only customer, and the improbably thin Hispanic girls behind the counter are yelling at each other. When they see Harry, they yell at Miller. "You can't bring no dog in here!"

"You know you can't bring no dog in here!" The girls are sisters, maybe twins, and they speak in echoes.

"Sorry," Miller says. "I just wanted an espresso. A quickie."

The prettier sister, with lustrous black hair and a silver stud in her tongue, shakes her head back and forth. "I can't give you nothing unless you take that dog outta here."

"Just an espresso," Miller says. "C'mon. It's been a day."

"It ain't been a day," the girl says. She puts her hands on her hips, flirting. "It's only been a morning, honey. And I got work to do. So don't waste my time whining—get that dog outta here and I'll get you some damn espresso." She's smiling wide. Her T-shirt, cut low on top and short on the bottom, says SUGAR on it. She's wearing tiny shorts and hoop earrings. Harry lies down on the bakery floor.

"Just an espresso," Miller says.

"Come on, baby," says the girl, still shaking her head, leaning over the counter. "Don't give me no hard time."

She puts her hand on the counter. Her nails are long and painted pearly white. Miller's breath whooshes out of him; he's falling in love.

"Give me a break," says the other sister, not quite as pretty and also less courageous—no stud in the tongue, no belly button. What she lacks in bravery she seems to exhibit in common sense. "Here's your espresso," she says. "A dollar eighty-five." She bumps her sister with her hip as she hands Miller the espresso from the other side of the counter. Miller's breath whooshes again; he is now in love with them both. He wants to stay in the bakery for the next hundred years. It occurs to him that he's never before slept with twins.

The prettier sister hands him fifteen cents. "But, no shit, you really gotta get that dog outta here. My boss'll lose his shit if he sees a dog."

"Department of Health," the other one says. Miller swallows his espresso in one gulp to try and impress them. They simultaneously roll their eyes.

"C'mon, Harry," he says, pulling on the dog's leash. "We're not wanted."

"*You're* wanted," says the prettier one. "It's the dog."

"The dog."

"Right," Miller says. He winks at both girls. He feels brazen, Casanova-ish, free. A flirt and an espresso. No wonder the Italians have such a capacity for joy. "See you later, ladies."

"See ya," they sing out together. When Miller walks out of the bakery, the warm smells of sugar and butter dissolve. The gray Brooklyn streets still smell like rain, even though it is no longer raining.

The Flood

Back in the apartment, Miller drops the dog's leash on the table in the front hall. Harry looks up at him and nuzzles his crotch; nice walk, old chum. Then the dog takes up residence on his cushion by the front windows. Miller pats him on the head, adjusts his glasses, and raps on the bathroom door. "So?" he says.

"How was your walk?" Lisa asks.

"It was fine," he says. "How was your pee?"

"Still working on it."

"Still?" he asks. "It's been twenty minutes."

"I guess I'm nervous."

"Nothing to be nervous about," he says. "It's a biological function."

"Maybe you could tell me a story," she says. "To help."

"Maybe you're joking."

"Miller!" she says. "Don't be a jerk."

Christ. The story trick is something she pulls on her first-graders. When a kid is sitting on the can complaining that "it won't come out," Lisa will actually sit there and tell him all about rushing rivers or flowing faucets or something of that ilk. She swears, to Miller, that it works.

"What do you want?" he asks. "A story about waterfalls?"

"Oh, good idea," Lisa says. He can see her in there, smiling, balancing on the can. He cringes. "Or a story about swimming pools," she continues. "Or floods."

"Lisa, you're not in the first grade."

"But I am," she says. "Nine months of the year."

"God. How's Noah's Ark?" It's the only flood story he can remember, and he's of no mind right now to come up with fresh material.

"Sounds perfect," she says.

He sits down in front of the bathroom door and crosses his legs. Harry shuffles over to sit sleepily beside him. Miller lights a Camel Light and tries to remember how the story goes.

"Once upon a time," he says, "there was a righteous man named Noah."

"I remember."

"A nice guy, a hard worker, prayed regularly at the temple. Had some kids. Three, I think. Sons." That's right, isn't it? Miller thinks. Three sons?

"Okay."

"And," he continues, "since Noah prayed, took care of his family, paid all his taxes, helped out his neighbors, God looked with favor upon him. God thought Noah was a deserving man. But the problem was, Noah lived and worked among complete assholes. Thieves, liars, backstabbers, cheaters. And all these assholes made God angry."

"Well, of course," Lisa says. "Old Testament."

"So God decided there was one way to deal with all the negative energy in Noah's neighborhood: wash away the problems with a big, cleansing flood."

"Ah."

"God spoke to Noah, said I want you to build a big old boat, fill it with two of every kind of animal you can find. And then I want you to put your family on that boat and watch out. It's gonna rain."

"Yessir."

"Rain like nobody's seen it before. Forty days and forty nights of gushing water, falling from the heavens. Water that could fill the oceans a hundred times over, spilling over everything, waves and waves of it. The water flows and runs and covers the towns and people and trees and buildings and all the forests of the earth. Water, water everywhere. Spilling, running," he says. "Can you imagine?"

"Oh, yes," she says.

"Water," Miller repeats. "Spilling and splashing, running and gushing, curtains of water dropping from the sky."

"Okay," Lisa says. "That did the trick." And then Miller can hear, through the locked bathroom door, his girlfriend start to pee. He's now glad he told the story. He likes results.

And it's time to start taking this test.

The Sweet Smell of Success

In the ninth grade, Grant Hershey asked Miller if he knew the best way a woman's pussy could smell. Miller had no idea, at that point, what the options were in terms of the smells of women's pussies—still, he shrugged and tried to look manly about it.

"Come on," Grant said. "Think about it, faggot. Think about pussy."

Grant lived down the street and was six months younger than Miller but had sprinted ahead in the puberty dash—by fourteen, he had luxuriant curls of hair under his arms and whiskers above his mouth, and a few bristly hairs under his chin, which he liked to pull at. He did well in school. He was captain of the junior varsity basketball team. Girls dug him, and why not? Grant was broad and deep-voiced and weighed two hundred pounds, and Miller knew for sure he'd stuck his fingers deep inside Jodie DiMarco, because he'd hid in Grant's closet and watched. They were best friends.

"So do you know? You know?"

"The best way pussy can smell?" Miller knew the lingo, at least: cunt, pussy, snatch, twat. Grant was leaning over him at his locker, waiting for him to pack up his books so that they could head out to The Hill, where Miller would smoke nervous cigarettes and Grant would make out with Jodie.

"Yeah. You know?"

Miller shrugged again. He himself longed for Jodie DiMarco in his most secret heart.

Grant leaned toward Miller, his breath smelling like stale Coca-Cola, his thick neck like Drakkar Noir. "Nothing," he whispered. "The best-smelling pussy smells like nothing at all."

Miller nodded. "Okay," he said. He wondered, at the time, if this bit of information would ever prove useful.

Although Miller has discarded most of the effects of his childhood: photographs, favorite books, northern New Jersey—he has held on to Grant Hershey for almost twenty years. Miller still enjoys Grant, or at least he thinks he does; by now he is so used to his friend's loudness and vulgarity and appetite that he's not sure whether or not he really likes Grant anymore or if he just needs to have him around, like cigarettes.

In his adult incarnation, Grant works as an investment banker and lives in a fine loft in Tribeca; he brags that his was the first building to install an automatic garbage disposal system after New York City decriminalized them a few years back. He is still traditionally handsome in a way that appeals to traditionally handsome women: he slicks back his black curls with gel that smells like Comet and wears shoes made from nearly extinct reptiles. Miller continues to be an audience for his information about, among other things, pussy. Several nights ago, they drank beers together in Grant's loft, the lights of his pinball machine blinking and glittering in the cool darkness.

"The smell of it," Grant said. He was lying on his goatskin couch and waving a cigarette in the air. This conversation was, in every respect, a continuation of the one they'd started fourteen years before, at Miller's locker. "It's the best way to know a woman," Grant said. He flicked ashes into the darkness of his apartment. "Smell her out."

"You'd think you'd grow up," Miller said. He was sitting on the floor, leaning back on his hands, a limey Corona between his legs.

"No, *you'd* think I'd grow up," Grant said. He sat up and

pointed at Miller with his cigarette. "I never harbored any illusions."

Miller sighed. He took a swig of his beer. "You know, there really are better ways to know a woman than to take off her underwear and smell."

"You're wrong, my friend."

"Conversation, maybe?"

"Nope. You're a nice guy, but you're wrong."

"Take her out for a nice meal?"

"Wrong, wrong, wrong." Grant jammed his cigarette into the glass ashtray on the floor beside the couch. He was, Miller knew, about to pontificate. It was a warm night outside, but cool inside the loft, and Miller considered—and was subtly pleased by—the fact that they'd been hashing this out for so many years. It was comforting, though by now there was really nowhere to advance.

Miller thinks: Lisa's pussy smells like the rest of her. This is to say clean, and occasionally pungent. Lisa's smell is totally her own. Sometimes it amazes Miller how she can be so unconcerned with cosmetics and perfumes, which does not mean she's a slob—she can be vain, even, about certain aspects of her appearance, especially her legs and breasts. She'll wear short shorts and go braless, and will sometimes spend the length of a television drama brushing out her long brown hair. But she doesn't waste too much time or money on fancy products because she has uncommon faith in her own beauty. As far as he can tell, she's the first woman he's ever known to have that sort of faith. He supposes that he likes it.

But Blair Carter was different, used Lily of the Valley perfume and vanilla bath salts, mocha-colored lip gloss and chamomile conditioner in her hair. Miller liked that too.

He has not spoken to Blair Carter in a year and a half, and it unnerves Miller how frequently he thinks about her, and it embarrasses him that Lisa knows. Lisa knows, or at least she suspects. It's the one thing she's not up-front about—she never asks Miller about Blair, or refers to anything that took place during the time he knew her. Miller tries not to mention Blair either, which leaves a hole.

"A woman who takes care of herself"—Grant was still pontificating—"a clean woman, a woman who likes to shower every day and maybe goes to the gym, she's going to smell like soap and water, right?" Grant said. "Maybe a little funk, but nothing too bad, nothing you can't stand. It'll even taste good if that's the sort of mood you're in. And you know you've got a woman who's proud of herself, a woman who respects herself, a woman who's not going to take any shit but who still likes men enough to want to clean up for them." To punctuate, Grant pressed PLAY on the stereo's remote. The room filled with Jay-Z.

"You're still listening to corporate rap?" said Miller, whose own musical tastes ran to good old-fashioned Motown, the rhythm and blues that his father used to play when he was happy.

"A woman who smells like raw funk, on the other hand. A woman who smells like old cheese . . ."

"Right, right." Miller lay back on the floor and stared up at Grant's ceiling.

"She doesn't shower all the time, right? She doesn't necessarily . . . *cleanse*. But she's hot, right? And you know that she's been with all your friends, and you don't care what she smells like—in a weird way the bad smell even turns you *on*, and you're thinking to yourself, this bitch is so dirty and I wish she weren't but I'm sort of glad she is, 'cause she's not going to expect anything of me, you know? She's been through it before. She knows what to do."

"Or maybe she has an infection," Miller said.

"I don't do chicks with infections."

"Don't you ever get bored with this, G?" Miller asked. He

poked at the lime in his Corona and grinned up at his old friend. "Doesn't this shit get stale?"

"Never, man," Grant said. He lay back on the couch, a shine in his eyes. "Never in a million years."

"What are you reading right now?" Miller asked. He needed to change the subject because he suddenly felt old.

"John Dos Passos," Grant said. "Trying to shut me up, huh?"

"It's getting late, man," Miller said. "It's late."

What Next?

He looks up at the clock, which hangs near the bathroom door. It's ten to twelve. Lisa's been in the bathroom for almost a half hour and he wonders what he's supposed to do now. He could run to the Clay Pot on Seventh Avenue and buy her an engagement ring. He could call Planned Parenthood and ask for advice. He has known Lisa for a little more than a year, but it occurs to him that he has not planned, does not plan, on having a future with her. After Blair, Miller decided not to do a lot of planning. But he had fallen in with Lisa, and they are comfortable, and he doesn't want that to change. How could they have let this happen?

Miller scratches Harry's head and thinks: *Lisa and I like each other and get along well and make terrific roommates. When we tell each other that we love each other, which we do only rarely, we both know what the other person means. That this is a friendly kind of love.*

He knocks on the door and Lisa knocks back. "So what's next?" he asks.

"With the pee?" she says. "Um . . . I'm supposed to stick a tab into it, you know, but I'm sort of leaning toward taking a bath."

"Where's the pee? What did you do with it?"

"It's on the counter," she says. "In its cup."

"So you're just going to take a bath with a cup of pee on the counter?" Miller finds this disgusting. Also, he is growing impatient.

"Pee is mostly water anyway," she says. "It's no big deal."

"Okay," Miller says. "Whatever."

"Don't whine," she says.

"Who's whining?" Well. Anyway, Miller knows that Lisa wipes up the pee of other people's children on an almost daily basis. She is conversant with snot, vomit, blood, and tears. Children are a liquidy bunch and Lisa is not afraid of any of it. She's even wiped her kids' asses when they've needed her to. But, Jesus. He wishes she would just stick Tab A, etcetera.

"So you're okay?" he asks her.

"Yeah, I'm okay," Lisa says. "Just thinking a lot."

"Right," he says, because after all it does seem right that Lisa should be thinking a lot. Fuck, he hasn't thought this hard in who knows how long. Miller wonders, though, why he doesn't want to ask Lisa exactly what she's thinking. And he wonders why she does not seem to want to ask him.

PART TWO

(Primarily Concerning Miller's Fourteenth Summer, and His Difficulties Managing Stan and Bay)

Physiognomy

Lisa and Miller's apartment is arranged like a T, with the kitchen and bedroom at either end and the living room at the stem; the bathroom juts off the hallway. The walls are thick with the coats of paint that have been applied for each new tenant over the years. The floors are scuffed wood. The doorknobs are prewar, old-fashioned crystal.

Miller has been spending a lot of time in the hallway this morning, but now he stands up and goes to the bedroom and takes a closer look in the mirror than he usually does. There are the standard things he checks for: nothing stuck between the teeth, no gray in the hair, no thinning toward the middle of his scalp. It's a relief. Miller looks like his mother, and in her family, men retain their hair well into their sixties. Stan, on the other hand, was as bald as a grapefruit by the time he was thirty-three.

Miller straightens his glasses and peers a little closer, looking for something unnameable. In the Victorian era, people were believers in the importance of physiognomy. They felt that by looking closely at someone else they could understand that person's character traits. Wide eyes signal wisdom, a bumpy nose reveals a sense of humor, full lips equal the capacity to betray. Miller studies his high cheekbones, round brown eyes, long skinny nose. He has his mother's face, and he thinks of it now; the crease between her eyes proved her constant anxiety, and the gap in her teeth revealed impatience. Miller has no crease between his eyes, and his teeth are all evenly spaced, so he assumes he'd be a more relaxed parent than his mother was. Or at least he hopes so.

The day after Stan left fifteen years ago, Bay awoke rejuvenated. In the preceding weeks, she'd been cheerless but subdued—Dr. Weintraub's newest drugs had calmed her down but kept her dull. And yet today here she was, cooking breakfast, looking comfortable in the kitchen. Miller was impressed. Maybe, he thought, Stan's absence was the medicine that would finally take.

"I'm making eggs, if you want," she said.

"For me?" he said.

"Don't be ungrateful." Her eyes, which lately had seemed unable to focus, were now alert behind turquoise-framed glasses. She was wearing a white blouse and she'd combed her hair. She spooned her eggs from the pan to a plate, pulled the toast from the toaster, sat down at the table, and started to eat.

"You're staring," she said, wiping her plate with the toast. "It's impolite."

Miller poured himself a bowl of Frosted Flakes and continued to regard his mother curiously. She chewed. A minute later, when he got up to pour himself some juice, he was further impressed. In the refrigerator was a carton of milk.

"Is this fresh?" he asked. Miller had, over the past year or so, become accustomed to eating his cereal dry. Bay had ceased to go grocery shopping and Stan, who could never quite remember Miller's requests, took to purchasing only the foods he himself found useful: bread, eggs, roast beef, grapefruit juice, tomatoes, garlic, spaghetti, ice cream. Chiles. Miller's father was not much of a cook, but he traveled a lot to Texas for business, and there he learned how to make a salsa so hot it could burn a hole through your tooth. He was quite proud of this salsa, and liked to spoon it on fried eggs, and eat it with tears leaking out of his eyes.

"I went grocery shopping this morning," Bay said. She spread the newspaper out in front of her, turned to the metro section. She was wearing orange lipstick. "I decided it was time to get this house in order, seeing as how it's just the two of us now." She winked at Miller. He took a step backward. "Time to turn this house into a home. You're sure you don't want any eggs?"

"I'm sure," he said. It was July, so there was no school to rescue him, but in the summer he could take his bike down to the community pool. "I'm gonna go swimming."

"Not today," his mother said.

"Why not?" he asked, a budding apprehension knotting his stomach. She had a glint in her eye. She was making plans.

"There's work to be done here." Bay smiled. Her orange lipstick had made its way to her teeth.

"You know, I don't think I can," Miller said. "I really have to get to the pool. Grant's going to be there, and Doug, and I promised them—"

"Promises, shmomises," she said. She stood up and wiped her hands on her skirt. "Those morons will survive without you. I need you here today. You're going to be my little helper, kiddo."

"No can do," Miller said. His mother rarely used the word *kiddo*. He continued to back up. He was clutching his bowl of Frosted Flakes.

"Who's in charge here?" Bay sang out, her voice getting higher.

"I promised," Miller said, "that I'd meet them at the pool. I'm gonna be late if I don't go. You know how Grant gets." He hoped he sounded like he meant it.

"There are some *things*," his mother said, eyes narrowing, "that we need to *accomplish*. In this *house*," she said. "*Today*."

She was angling herself around the kitchen table, walking slowly toward him. She, too, was holding her plate.

"But I . . ." he started. Miller was now standing in the hall. He put his cereal down on the floor.

"But nothing," his mother said. She dropped her own plate on the counter by the kitchen door; like a cornered animal, Miller felt his blood vessels dilate and the adrenaline begin to course. Her eyes were off him for perhaps three seconds while she deposited her dish, and he took those three seconds for the opportunity they were. He started to run. Miller scrambled up the stairs, keeping a low center of gravity, using his arms to propel himself forward while his legs jumped three steps at a time. He could hear his mother behind him, but she was wearing high heels (heels!) and was anyway nowhere near as fast.

"Joel!" she said. "Joel! You stop where you are! We're cleaning this house today!" Bay was a heavy smoker and was out of breath by the top stair. He dashed down the hall and into his father's old study, where he slammed the door and planted himself behind it. He knew his mother hated going into his father's study, but just to be safe he twisted the lock.

"Joel Miller," she said. She was standing directly on the other side, and he could hear her panting for air. "I just want your help . . . help cleaning the house today . . . I don't think it's too much to ask."

He kept silent. He looked around the room where his father had lately been spending so much time. The green leather seat of his chair was still imprinted with the fat twin loaves of his ass, and the air smelled like his sweat.

"Joel," she growled. He pressed his back against the door. Stan had left so much behind. The framed baseball programs, the ticket stubs to a hundred games at Shea, the signed and mounted baseball from the 1973 World Series, which the Mets had lost. Pamphlets from Holland Pharmaceuticals, where he'd worked the past twenty-five years. Diplomas. An old stack of *Playboys* half-hidden under the desk. And a picture of Bay, when she was younger and beautiful, framed on the desk. Miller picked it up.

"Look," she said, on the other side of the door, "nobody likes to clean. I know how it is. I *hate* to clean, personally. But I think we need a fresh start, a new start in this house. . . . I think we need a . . ."

His mother's hair once lay flat against her head. She'd even maintained some wispy bangs. The skin around her eyes had been smooth, and her smile was open and graceful. She was probably about twenty-seven in this picture. Miller was born when she was thirty-five.

"Joel," she said, and he could hear the familiar, irresistible sadness in her voice. He opened the door. She was leaning against the door frame.

He held out the picture so she could see. "This was you," he said.

"Joel." She sounded weak and a little angry, but she took the picture from Miller and held it in both hands. "Where was this?" she asked.

"On his desk."

She nodded and looked at it once more. "What's your point?" she said, although it didn't sound to Miller like a question. She glanced down at herself, her skirt, her knobby knees. "I guess I was prettier then," she sighed. "But everybody gets older."

He shrugged, and she turned to him and fluffed his hair. "Don't be smug. You'll be an old man too, someday." She handed the picture back. "Put it where you found it."

Miller did as he was told. She lifted her turquoise eyeglasses and rubbed her eye with the heel of her left hand. "I'm trying to get better, you know," she said. "Don't make me feel worse about it."

"Look, did you stop taking your medicine, and were you supposed to, and don't you think you should call Dr. Weintraub?" Miller asked. He couldn't help himself.

"Excuse me?" Bay said. "Did I what?"

"You know," Miller said. It made him so weary, her medicine, this conversation, his father's abandoned study. "Don't you need that medicine Dr. Weintraub gave you?"

"Hey, don't worry about me," Bay said. "I'm fine now, really. I'm taking good care of myself. You can't help me by worrying about me."

Well, of course Miller knew this, because he'd been worrying for almost three years now and it hadn't helped one bit.

"C'mon," Bay said. "I think it's time we cleaned up this house. I'm not kidding."

Then she disappeared down the hall.

Miller stuffed a *Playboy* from his father's stash under his shirt and followed.

Protection

Grant was concerned. High school would start in a mere two months, transferring them from the gentle backwater of Heyward Junior to the terrifying cosmopolis of Heyward–Demarrey Valley Regional Senior High School. Demarrey Valley bordered Heyward on the northern, southern, and western sides, much as Germany had surrounded Poland just before World War II. Years ago, the valley was where the lucky few living on Heyward's verdant hillsides had housed their domestic servants. Although the traditional hilltop-valley distribution of wealth was no longer as rigid as it once was, previous inequities had generated certain long-term consequences. For instance, the houses in Heyward were large colonials, while the houses in the valley were more ramshackle, and the children from Heyward tended to be milder sorts, while the valley children were bigger, hairier, and generally not nearly as afraid to skin their knees.

"We're gonna be killed," Grant said.

"We are not," Miller said. They were sitting in Miller's backyard, dipping their toes in the icy creek.

"I wish my parents would pay for private school," Grant said. It was Grant's dear conviction that his parents were the cheapest people ever to have set foot in New Jersey, mostly because that they refused to get cable installed.

"Private school sucks," Miller said.

"What do you know?"

"What do you mean, what do I know?" From first through sixth grades, Miller had attended the Heyward Reserve Boys Academy. This was while Bay still worked a full-time job to pay for her social aspirations; once she quit the job and gave up going outside, she also stopped caring whether or not her son went to the "fancy" school. Miller gleefully burned his starchy green Heyward Reserve tie, and went to his first day in public school in cutoffs and an AC/DC T-shirt. Bay was catatonic in the guest room and didn't notice.

"Look," Grant said, kicking his feet back and forth in the creek. "I don't want to be a dick about it or anything, but you, specifically, are going to be butchered in high school. You weigh like, what, ninety pounds?"

"That's bullshit," Miller said, although in truth ninety pounds didn't sound that far off the mark.

"You should start eating more or something. You should lift some weights."

"It's my genes," Miller said. "I can't help it."

"Well, I'm just saying you should start beefing the fuck up. There's no way I'm getting my ass kicked on your behalf next year."

"That's kind of you." Miller saw a turtle poke its head up out of the creek, down about twenty feet from where they sat. The turtle filled him with the spontaneous joy that often accompanies the spotting of unexpected wildlife, but then, an instant later, he worried that the ability to feel such unalloyed joy might somehow make him a pussy. "You know what we could do that might help?" Miller said, turning away from the turtle. "We could start smoking. Nobody fucks with smokers."

Grant kicked at the water. "That's not a bad idea, son. How are we gonna score cigarettes?"

"We'll steal my mom's." What he didn't tell Grant was that he'd already begun smoking that year, in private, stealing packs of Virginia Slims out of his mother's cartons and relying on her absentmindedness to keep him out of trouble.

Grant nodded and stared off into the distance, as if reflecting. A moment later, a gleeful smile blossomed on his face. "Miller!" he said, pointing down the stream. "Check it out! A turtle!"

• • •

They crept into Bay's bedroom while she sat downstairs, watching television in her bathrobe. Miller made Grant perform surveillance outside while he retrieved a pack of Slims from her sock drawer. Once the cigarettes were secured, the boys barreled back down the stairs, but they were stopped, stilled, by a loud, miserable wail from the living room.

"What the fuck is that?" Grant asked.

Miller stuck the pack of cigarettes into the waistband of his shorts and cocked his ear. "Huh," he said. "Maybe we should wait this out upstairs."

"Dude, is that your mother?"

"Yeah." Miller fingered the pack of cigarettes hidden next to his skin. "I guess."

The wailing grew louder, filling the house with a ghostly, animal sound.

"Jesus, man," Grant said. "Maybe we should put back her cigarettes."

Miller shrugged. It all seemed so hopeless.

"What's your mom's problem, anyway?" Grant asked.

What's her problem? How to explain? Miller couldn't remember which had come first: his father's extended business trips or his mother's weeping fits on the couch. Stan would travel from Texas to Pennsylvania hawking pharmaceuticals; his mother would fill the space he left with frantic cleaning or cooking or buying new shoes. But then, more and more often, Bay would kiss Stan good-bye and then do nothing but cry, and Stan began to stay away longer. Fists clenched, Bay would hurl accusations at her nomadic husband whenever he reappeared: "You want me dead, you want to kill me, you never loved me at all."

Grant sat down on a step, wincing as Bay continued to keen. "What's she saying? 'Can't'? 'Can't'?"

Miller sat down next to Grant. "No," he said. "She's saying 'Stan.' "

Trouble Man

But then, a few days later, Bay made fried chicken for dinner. Made. Not ordered, not brought home in a bucket. Miller came home from the community pool and saw her standing in the kitchen, dipping fleshy pieces of chicken into a blue bowl full of flour. Marvin Gaye was on the stereo: "Trouble Man," which was the song his father used to listen to when he made his Texas salsa.

"What are you doing?" Miller asked, staring.

"Go take a shower," Bay said. "I can smell the chlorine from here." She was wearing old blue jeans and swinging her hips to the music as she dipped her pieces of chicken.

"But what are you doing?"

"I'm frying chicken." Bay spoke casually enough to suggest she fried chicken most evenings, before the seven o'clock news.

"You know how to fry a chicken?" Miller asked, amazed.

"You wanna help?" Bay asked.

Miller dropped his bag on the floor and stood next to her.

"First thing, wash your hands," she said, and Miller obliged. "Okay, now, I want you to carefully—*carefully*—roll pieces of chicken in the flour. You want to try for an even coat, not too thick, but make sure to get the flour all over the chicken. Shake the piece out over this plate. Then hand it to me. Can you do that?"

"Of course." "Trouble Man" switched over to "My Mistake," a duet with Diana Ross that he liked almost as much. He dipped the chicken in time with the music, and mouthed along to the words. He and his mother created an assembly line: Miller dipped, shook, and handed over; Bay dropped in oil, turned, and drained on pieces of paper towel. After "My Mistake" came "How Sweet It Is," then "Mercy Mercy Me," then "I Heard It Through the Grapevine," and then "What's Going On." When the tape turned to "You're All I Need to Get By," all the chicken was fried, and the kitchen smelled the way kitchens smelled in Miller's dreams.

Haircut

But that night, Miller had a nightmare. He dreamed that his mother was at the kitchen table, sliding knives in and out of their heavy wooden storage block. He had come downstairs to find her sitting there, under a greenish glow from the lamp that swung above her head. She was sliding those knives around and humming.

"Mom?"

She didn't answer. Her hair was tied up in a bandanna, and she wore a Rutgers sweatshirt and frayed sweatpants. Her eyes had thick black circles underneath them, as though she were a football player trying to find relief from the sun. She slid the knives mechanically, the paring knives, the chef's knife, the butcher.

"Mom?"

In his dream, Miller was wearing the private school uniform from Heyward Reserve: dark pants, a white shirt, a green tie. He could feel his hair pasted down to his head with sticky pomade.

"Mom?"

"Don't talk to me, Joel!" she shrieked. "I'm concentrating!"

Slide in. Slide out.

In his dream, Miller knew that he wanted to leave the kitchen. He could feel himself trying to force his legs to move the other way. And yet his legs were disobedient; they kept pushing him forward, toward the chair opposite Bay's at the kitchen table. His legs sat him down. His legs crossed at the ankles.

"You shouldn't be here." Bay was concentrating on the butcher knife, sliding it out, running her index finger along the edge, sliding it back into the block. "I mean it. You should be in bed."

"I know." He was hypnotized. "But what if you hurt yourself?"

"What are you going to do about it?" Bay asked. She held the butcher knife up to the greenish light.

"Please don't," Miller said. "I won't know what to do if you cut yourself."

Bay just sighed and then she did what Miller knew she would do the whole time. She took the knife and drew it casually across her wrist. Beads of blood sprang to the surface of her skin and ran together in a delicate tributary that flowed to the kitchen table. He looked up at her face, and saw that she was grimacing in pain.

He wanted to run away, but his legs wouldn't move.

When he woke up, his sheets were warm and damp; he had wet his bed again. The first time it happened was three years earlier, the night after he'd caught his mother in the bathroom slicing her hair off with one of the sharp thin knives from the block. Most of her hair already rested in skimpy piles around her bare veiny feet, lying on the bath mat like burned hay. Stan was in Phoenix. Miller had just come home from soccer practice, and ran into the bathroom to pee. For a second, he didn't even notice she was there.

He zipped himself up and blinked. "What are you doing?"

"Haircut," she said. She sliced through a lock of hair with a quick, scythe-like stroke.

"Why don't you use a scissors?" Miller asked, confused.

"I don't feel like it." She cut another piece of hair. He was afraid. Rather than ask any more questions, he simply closed the bathroom door and hurried away. When he saw her later that evening, practically bald, smoking in front of the television with tears on her cheeks, he told her that she looked pretty. He thought that might make her feel better.

Really, he felt ashamed.

In those days, a fifth-grader, Miller was a bit quiet, a bit lonely, a bit too anxious about how well he was fitting in. He was terrified of what might happen if a friend or neighbor saw his mother there, smoking, looking like one of the Holocaust survivors he'd learned about in history. Too thin, too ragged. Bald. What would they think of her? What would they think of him? And yet he couldn't be alone with her. What if she didn't stop crying? What if she did something worse?

That night, Miller stayed up until two in the morning, long after his mother had fallen asleep on the couch. He kept the cordless phone on his lap, hoping that his father would call. He didn't call often. But maybe he would. Miller knew about the time difference. It was earlier in Arizona. Maybe Stan would call. Maybe he'd know they needed him.

At two in the morning, Miller's eyes were chalky and dry. He had to go to sleep. And in the morning, when he was awoken by the ringing phone, he was too disoriented to realize why his legs were sticky and the sheets were wet and cold. His father was calling from Phoenix, but Miller couldn't bring himself to tell him what Bay had done. Stanley was too late.

Now, three years later, Miller woke up soaked again. His face burned; he'd thought this wouldn't happen anymore. He threw off his pajamas, threw his sheets in the washing machine, took a shower, and tucked himself into the spare bedroom. For a little while, he read a collection of Calvin and Hobbes cartoons that his mother kept there, but the problems of an imaginary tiger perversely compounded his own worries, and so after several pages he put the book down. Sleep still did not seem possible.

He crept down the hall to his mother's bedroom. Miller peeked in, his own heart beating anxiously. Yet why should he see anything different in there? What could possibly be wrong? And sure enough, when he looked at his mother on the bed, her eyes were closed, and she was gently snoring.

Just Desserts

A few weeks after that, Miller and his father sat at the Cliffs Diner near the entrance to the Palisades Parkway, eating apple pie and discussing his graduation from Heyward Junior.

"High school," Stan said. "About time, right?"

"I guess," Miller said. The truth was, he hadn't minded junior high. He'd gotten As in most classes, save wood shop and art, and hung around with the cool kids: Grant and Doug Becker and Jodie DiMarco. Better yet, Miller had been allowed on the baseball team. Even though he could barely hit an overhand pitch, Miller was the only boy in the eighth grade who loved the game enough to suffer the indignities of right field. But he knew there'd be no way he'd get to play for Heyward–Demarrey Valley, stocked as it was with players who could actually hit, run, and catch, players who were actually *good* at playing right field.

Stan swallowed a spoonful of pie. "You should know that your mother and I are both very proud of you."

"Not that much to be proud of," Miller said. "Any idiot could graduate from the eighth grade."

"I guess you've got a point there."

They ate quietly for a while: pie and coffee and french fries and bowls of whipped cream. Periodically Stan would offer a new topic of discussion: the high school basketball team, potential high school girlfriends, his own school memories of baseball and football and track, each of which he'd once played with enthusiasm if not actual prowess. Stan had graduated high school and gone on to Rutgers with dreams of making a team, any team. Sadly, neither hockey nor rugby nor basketball needed a squat nearsighted freshman with a bad arm, and anyway, soon enough Stan was distracted by a pretty girl named Bay, who wanted him to get an MBA and work for the pharmaceutical company that had held her own father in its employ for so many years.

"How is your mother, anyway?" Stan asked.

"She seems okay, I guess," Miller said. "Less tired all the time."

"She's trying to do a hell of a job," Stan said. "Pulling yourself out of the pits isn't easy." He wiped whipped cream off his mustache and then licked his fingers.

"I hope she keeps doing okay," Miller said. "I'm sick of worrying about her."

"Sure you are."

"It's hard to worry about someone all the time."

His father rubbed at his bald spot and asked the waitress for more pie. Miller, disgusted by his father's voracity, was drinking his coffee black.

"Well, you've been quite a man about everything," Stan said, after the waitress disappeared.

"Huh?"

"Listen," Stan said. "Let me tell you a little secret. Your mother loved me. Too much, maybe. Put me on a pedestal and didn't understand what I was and was not capable of. Didn't get my limits. She let me disappoint her all the time. What she failed to understand is that I'm a limited guy. A limited guy!" he said. He pounded on his chest for emphasis. "Limited! A complete failure in many ways!"

"Dad," Miller said. "Cut it out."

"A failed husband! A failed father!"

"Stop it," he said.

"Do you think I'm a failed father, son?" Stan asked him.

"You're the best father I've got," Miller said. They'd been through this before. Stan beamed.

"Waitress!" he called out, after beaming for a dozen more seconds. "A side of whipped cream, if you don't mind. And another cup of coffee for the boy."

Mothers Are Women Too

Bay's interest in fashion kept pace with her emotional stability. In times of stress, she retreated to the comfort of old sweatshirts and gym shorts, or Stan's enormous stained undershirts and tights. Sometimes she'd wrap a cardigan around herself, and pin back her hair with bobby pins or paper clips. The effect was melancholy but also youthful, somehow, and pretty.

When Bay was pulling it together, however, she took pains with her appearance, wearing lipstick and trying to keep her hair in some sort of order. She favored sweaters with sequined detailing and blouses printed with large, whimsical flowers. She wore her turquoise glasses and would sometimes peer over them to gauge her son's appearance. "Joel, my angel," she said to him on the last Saturday in July, once again mysteriously cheerful. "You're a man now. You're almost in high school. You're too old to keep dressing in filth."

Miller was eating his cereal—with milk—and reading the sports page and trying to ignore his mother.

"Did you hear me?" Bay demanded. She yanked the sports page away from under Miller's bowl, splashing him.

"Why are you always insulting me?" Miller howled. "Why can't I eat my breakfast in peace?"

"You sound like your father," Bay said. She sat back and folded her arms, peering critically at Miller. "I'm taking you shopping," she said.

"I'm on vacation. Leave me alone."

"Your shirt is too small. You're busting out of it. And those pants you wear are an embarrassment. To the mall we go."

"Can I at least finish my breakfast?"

"Time's a-wasting," Bay said, picking up her purse off the kitchen counter. "Besides, you don't need any more of that Frosted Flakes crap. It'll make you break out. And then who's gonna love you? Not me, I'll tell you that." But she grabbed Miller—already three inches taller than she was—around the shoulders and planted a fat kiss on his cheek. Miller couldn't help but smile, because his mother seemed happy.

They went to the Gap in Paramus Park. The clothing there was boring, but at least they could agree on it: jeans, T-shirts, a thick braided brown belt. "You should learn from your father," Bay said, holding a pile of cotton sweaters in primary colors. "He's a snazzy dresser." The air-conditioning was too high in the fluorescent-lit store and Bay had goose bumps on her arms.

"My father?" Miller stood in front of a mirror tacked to the wall. He was trying on a gray sweater over his T-shirt while attempting not to notice the salesgirl with the huge breasts standing a few feet away.

"You bet," Bay said. "I mean, not anymore, not since he, you know, got a little tubby, but once upon a time that man knew how to clean himself up."

Miller rolled his eyes. Lately, Bay was talking about Stan all the time, finding any excuse to work him into the conversation: Warm outside? Stan used to make the best lemonade on hot days; the secret was a little mint. Grant's parents got a new car? Oh, Stan loves new cars. Remember how excited he was when he bought the Caddy?

"I don't remember dad ever dressing like anything in particular."

"Trust me," Bay said. "He was a killer."

The salesgirl with the breasts came up to Miller and his mother, and Miller felt his pants start to swell. He positioned himself behind a pile of sweatshirts.

"You finding everything all right?" she asked.

"My boy," Bay said, "needs to work on his act a little, you know what I mean?"

"Work on his act?" The girl had the faintest tease of a New Jersey accent, a softening of the *r* in *work*, a hardening of the *t*.

"I'm seeing him in more khaki," Bay said. "Maybe a little rust."

"I'm not sure what we have in rust." The salesgirl looked apologetic. "We haven't done rust in a while, to be honest. This season it's a lot of brights. Primaries."

"No rust?" Bay asked. "Something maybe in tan?"

The girl shrugged, slightly at sea, and her T-shirt slipped to reveal the pale scalloped edge of her bra strap.

"Brights aren't rust, mom," Miller said, suddenly anxious to be part of the conversation.

"But I just think a color like that, you know, it would bring out your eyes. You have such beautiful brown eyes."

"He does have nice eyes." The girl smiled with more confidence, while Miller shifted his pants around a little, starting to panic.

"Listen, see what you can dig up in some khaki pants, size— What are you these days, honey? Maybe a twenty-nine? He's tiny, my son."

"Like his mother," the girl said. "I'll be right back." And

when she swished away toward the back of the store, Miller thought he might die.

"I can't believe you called me tiny. What's the matter with you?"

"It's not true?" Bay said. She was smiling with pleasure at being pronounced "tiny" herself.

"It's humiliating," Miller growled. He reached into the rack and pulled out a black cotton jacket. "It's not cool."

"Since when have I been cool?" She attempted to give him a hug, but Miller shifted out of her reach.

"Plus, I've been getting taller, just so you know," he muttered, trying to make his voice as icy as possible.

"I know," Bay said. "You think I don't notice? I can't even believe how handsome you are. I look at you and I can't even believe it, and that's the truth."

Miller jammed his arms into the jacket. He was boiling inside, a frothy stew of hormones and anger and a strange, misty sadness. He could not look at Bay.

"Hey," she said. "Hey, listen to me. I don't mean to embarrass you. But it's true, you should dress nicely, you've gotten so handsome these days."

"Would you stop it? Please?" He looked at himself once more in the mirror, his eyes narrowing, his shoulders forward.

"I've upset you," Bay said. "Oh, honey, I'm so sorry. I didn't mean to—"

"You just don't know anything, mom," Miller hissed. "You don't know a goddamn thing."

And ordinarily Bay would smack him in the face for cursing—a bit of hypocrisy Miller never knew how to protest—or scream right back. But there, for the first time, Miller recognized that he was taller than she was, and probably stronger, and he knew she wouldn't dare. And she didn't. Instead, she put her hands over her eyes and took a long, shuddering breath. "I'm so sorry," she said again. "I didn't mean to embarrass you, honey; I really didn't."

"All right, mom." He could feel his anger begin to unclench, like a fist after a punch has been thrown. He turned away from his reflection.

"I'm sorry."

"It's okay," Miller said. "Enough."

A few moments later the girl reappeared, holding three pairs of neatly folded khaki pants against her bosom. "Why don't you try these on? I got you a twenty-nine, but also a thirty, just in case. You don't look all *that* tiny to me."

Miller reached out and took the pants from the girl's hands. "Okay," he said softly. The girl smiled at him and bit her shiny lower lip. Miller's stomach twisted. For the first time in his life, suddenly and sharply, he had fallen in love. It lasted for three sore-armed days, until time, as it will, stripped those tender feelings away.

Off-Season

Grant was going to St. Maarten with his family during the first two weeks in August. "Cheap fucks," he said. "Of course we've got to go during the *off-season;* of course they're not going to pay for us to go to the Caribbean when normal people go."

"When do normal people go to the Caribbean?" Miller asked. They were practicing smoking by the creek. Grant, to Miller's delight, was terrible at it. He could barely manage to inhale without coughing like an emphysemiac.

"The winter," Grant said, throwing his cigarette butt into the creek. "Smoking sucks," he said. "It would be better to lift weights or something."

Miller leaned against the tree, grasping his cigarette between his thumb and one finger, imagining himself James Dean incarnate. "Only retards lift weights."

"You think you're one cool motherfucker, don't you?" Grant said.

"You kiss your mother with that mouth?"

Grant spat into the creek and took out another cigarette, propping it between his pursed lips. Miller lit it for him with a match from a restaurant matchbook.

"Listen, I just don't want you freaking out or anything while I'm gone," Grant said, after he'd finally inhaled and exhaled successfully. "I was thinking"—he paused for a second—"I mean, do what you want, but I was thinking that maybe you should go stay with your dad for the rest of the summer."

"What are you talking about?"

"I don't know," Grant said. He sat down at the trunk of the old maple that used to serve as first base when Miller and his father played softball. "I'm just not sure you should stay trapped with your mother all summer. What if she completely flips out and tries to kill you or something?"

Miller slid down against the tree he'd been leaning on. "Fuck you, Grant."

"No, man, I'm not trying to . . . It's just that she's been so psycho lately—"

"Grant . . ." Miller said.

"Look, I'm only saying it"—and here Grant put his hand on his heart and batted his eyelashes like a girl—"because I care."

"My mother's not going to flip out."

"What's she doing right now?"

"Probably sleeping," Miller said. "She's not psycho anymore. She's just usually tired." In fact, Miller suspected that, although he couldn't find her pill bottle, Bay had started to take Dr. Weintraub's medicine again, because she was taking long naps in the middle of the afternoon and seemed, in her waking hours, to be relatively calm.

"Well, if she's sleeping . . ." Grant said. "Whatever." He picked up a twig and started scraping it against the ground.

"What I mean is, she's getting better. She's trying to get better."

"Dude, it's cool." Grant bent the twig against the ground

until it snapped. "If you think everything's fine, then everything's fine."

"It's not that I think everything's fine . . ." Miller said, and then stopped, unsure how to explain. He stubbed out his cigarette against the bottom of his sneaker and sighed. "I just don't think going to my dad's house will do anything to make it better."

"Okay," Grant said. He looked away again, but it seemed to Miller that his friend was uncomfortable. On a clinical level, Miller was impressed, because it was rare to catch Grant in an awkward moment.

"I mean, it's nice of you to be worried or whatever . . ." Miller started.

"I wasn't worried, you faggot," Grant said. "Pass me another cigarette and shut up."

"Opposition Is True Friendship"

Or so said William Blake; Miller found that quote in *Bartlett's Familiar Quotations* and had it inscribed under his picture in his high school yearbook. By sheer coincidence, Grant also used Blake ("No bird soars too high if he soars with his own wings"), which confirmed, in Miller's mind, that he and his friend were cosmically linked. He was probably right. In the eleven years since high school, Grant and Miller's friendship has remained constant, and therefore it is no surprise that Grant calls on this soggy April Saturday just as Miller is about to freak out: Lisa is still locked in the bathroom. Harry's asleep on the floor.

"Pregnancy scare, huh?" It turns out Grant's calling from a sport boat off the coast of Miami, a little last-minute deep-sea fishing. "Man, I remember my first pregnancy scare. Carrie Braffitt, remember her? Back at Columbia? With the tits?"

"Carrie Braffitt—wasn't she a little crazy?" Miller says. He is so grateful to hear from Grant. He takes the phone with him to the kitchen, pours himself a beer.

"Yeah, a nut job. Catholic. This one time her period was late and she was like, you're gonna marry me, you asshole. I said, hey, princess, let's not get ahead of ourselves." Grant chuckles at the memory. "Of course, when it came down to it, she decided to get an abortion in five minutes flat. Not even Carrie Braffitt was crazy enough to want to marry *me*."

"Yeah, I remember. Didn't she want you to go to confession with her after it was all over?"

"Confession! Hell, she wanted me to get *castrated*." Miller can hear seagulls cawing on Grant's end of the line. "I hear she's like a district attorney out in L.A. these days. Sends drunk drivers to the pen. It makes sense."

"So how did you feel about that whole abortion thing after it was over?" Miller asks. He sits down at the kitchen table, sips his beer. "You didn't really talk about it much."

"You know, mostly relieved, I guess. Maybe a little guilty, but mostly relieved." The boat's horn blares. "Who wants to be a father at nineteen? Anyway, you should see it down here, kid. The sun's shining, it's eighty-nine degrees, not a cloud—"

"I don't know what I'll do," Miller says. "If she's pregnant. I really don't know what I'll do."

"Well . . ." Miller can hear him inhaling on a cigarette. "It's sort of not up to you." Grant pauses. "You can stay with her or you can leave her, but whether or not she has the baby—that's pretty much her choice. You can't tell her to have it if she doesn't want to have it, and you can't tell her to get rid of it if, worst-case scenario, she wants it. Fathers are peripheral, you know. Motherhood's where the action's at."

"So I have no say?"

"Not exactly," Grant says. "You've just got to know your place." In the background, the horn blares again.

"Are you heading out to sea?" Miller says, just before static overtakes their connection. "Thanks for the thoughts." And with that, they're disconnected. Grant is after the fish.

"Who called?" Lisa asks from the other side of the bathroom door.

"Grant. He's in Miami. Deep-sea fishing. Just decided to take off for the weekend."

"He give you any good advice?"

Miller pauses, drains his beer. "He says that you're the one in charge here."

In the living room, the old wooden clock emits a surprisingly loud click. The clock is quirky—it was Lisa's grandmother's—and its unpredictable tick can be nerve-racking. Harry leaps up. "Funny," Lisa says, "I don't feel very in charge."

"Neither do I," Miller says. He resumes his old position, cross-legged outside the bathroom door.

"So maybe we should just let fate be in charge," Lisa says. Miller thinks, Fate's already done its job. Fate has nothing left to do.

"Listen," he says. "Will you just take this test already?" On the other side of the door, there's nothing but silence.

Visitation

Bay's stability continued to wax and wane during the course of Miller's fourteenth summer. One evening in August, she sang along with the Beach Boys while she mopped the floor, but the next morning she sat at the kitchen table and picked furiously at her cuticles as Miller ate a breakfast of Pop-Tarts with chocolate sauce. It was ten in the morning and ninety-four degrees outside. "So why aren't you at the pool?" she asked. "Where's your partner in crime?"

"He went to St. Maarten," Miller said, and when Bay looked at him quizzically he continued. "It's 'cause his parents are cheap and they only want to pay to go during the off-season."

"Grant's parents aren't cheap," Bay said. Her fingers were bloody where the skin met the nail. "The Hersheys are lovely people. They have a lovely family." She liked Grant's family because his mother was slim and pretty and his father was a cardiologist.

"I guess," Miller said. He couldn't bear to watch Bay tear at her hands. He went over to the refrigerator, opened it, silently cataloged the contents.

"It would be so nice if we could go on a vacation," Bay said. "Me and you and your father. Like we used to. Maybe down to the shore."

"I don't remember going to the shore," Miller said, looking fixedly at a Tupperware container full of rotting salad.

"You were a baby," Bay said. "You'd run around on the beach like a little naked button."

"Nice," Miller said. He closed the refrigerator door.

"I'm going to talk to your father about it."

That Saturday, when Stan pulled up in the Cadillac, Bay hopped off the steps and rushed to his car window like a waitress at a drive-in. She had dressed up for Stan's arrival, putting on the lipstick, patting down the hair, but the heat wave lingered and her face was shiny with sweat. "I have an idea!" she said, as Miller followed behind her. "It's the best idea. We're going to take a vacation together. The three of us."

"Where are we going?" Stan said, turning down the car radio. Miller slid into the seat next to his father, thrilling to the powerful AC.

"Down the shore," Bay said. "Like we used to."

"We haven't been down the shore in eleven years," Stan said.

"We'll use Carol's house," Bay said. Carol was a physician's assistant at the office where Bay used to work. "I know she'll let us. Next weekend. Come on, it'll be fun!" She was smiling, not a crazy smile, no lipstick on her teeth—just pure and wide-eyed and excited. The combination of the heat and Bay's excitement was a force too powerful to resist. Miller nudged his father in the side.

"Why don't you call me this week," Stan said. "Maybe we can figure something out."

Later that afternoon, watching the Mets lose to the Cardinals at Shea, Miller asked his father if he thought a trip to the shore was a good idea.

"Son," Stan said, swirling the remains of a light beer in a plastic cup, "I haven't seen your mother look that happy about a plan in years, I tell you. Years."

"But do you think we'd all get along?" Miller asked, fanning himself with a scorecard.

"Haven't we been talking about this?" Stan said. "How well she's doing?"

"Yeah, but do you think she'll do that well if all three of us are together? Do you think maybe she'll crack up again?"

"Listen," Stan said. "I've got a lot going on right now." He paused and looked into his beer again, as if seeking guidance. "What I mean to say is"—he paused—"there's a lot. Going on. And so, if I can make your mother smile for a minute or two, make her happy—well, that's one less thing I've got to worry about. She's a lot easier to please," Stan added, "than she used to be."

Miller fidgeted in his seat. He watched Gary Carter swing once, twice, three times, go back to the dugout. "I just have a bad feeling," he said.

"Jesus, son, why do you sound so nervous?" Stan asked. "You sound like a goddamn weenie."

"I sound like a what?" Miller asked. Well, sure, he knew he sounded like a weenie, but while living alone with Bay was fraught, he preferred it to the experience of living with both his parents together; the thought of a return to previous conditions made his stomach hurt.

"You sound," Stan said grandly, "like a good goddamn weenie."

"Dad," said Miller, "what kind of a weenie uses the word *weenie?*"

Stan laughed and punched his son on the shoulder. He was cheerful. They had good seats, really excellent, right over the visitors' dugout, a gift from Holland Pharmaceuticals. "I could use a vacation myself," he said. "It'll be very refreshing. I'm sure the three of us will get along fine. We're civilized people."

"Are we?"

Stan flagged down a vendor and ordered another beer. "Well, I am," he said. "And you are. And as for your mother, we'll do what we always do." He passed the vendor a five-dollar bill and reached out for a brand-new beer. "Close our eyes and cross our fingers and pray for the goddamn best."

Down the Shore

Carol's tiny house in Ocean City was all plank-board and nautical notions, fishing nets tacked to the wall above the television and a life-size plastic sailfish glued to the wall above the kitchen table. Carol and her husband came down to this house most summer weekends with their small twin daughters, but this weekend they were vacationing in Disney World. Miller was to stay in the girls' room, at the end of the hall, with frilly pink beds and an array of stuffed animals, which had stiffened in the salty air.

"Heaven!" Bay said, twirling around on the front porch. The house was a block away from the ocean. "Is this heaven or what, boys?" Stan, his belly wrapped tight in a Mets T-shirt, popped open two beers and handed one to Bay.

"Heaven," he agreed. "Want a beer, son?"

Miller looked down. His stomach had started to burn this morning and wouldn't stop.

"Why are you so quiet?" Bay asked.

"He's been like this all day. Have a beer, son."

"I don't want a beer," Miller said. "Thanks, though."

"What kind of kid says no to beer? Bay, what are you teaching my son?"

Bay giggled and kissed Stan on the cheek. They were standing by the rail of the porch, and Miller watched them toss back their beers and giggle together. He was sitting behind them, against the wall of the house, and could see Bay's vein-crossed legs emerging from her short blue shorts, and Stan's back jiggling as he laughed. They had their arms around each other.

"I'm too young to drink beer," Miller muttered, just loud enough for his parents to hear.

"What did you say?" Bay asked.

"I'm too young to drink beer!" Miller shouted, possessed by an energy that seemed to come from nowhere. "You should know that! I'm fourteen years old! What kind of parents would give their fourteen-year-old beer?" He could feel his fists clench in his lap.

"Easy there," Stan said, turning around. "I was just kidding with you, son."

Bay turned too, and leaned her head on Stan's shoulder. "What's with the shouting?"

"I'm not shouting," Miller said, and he wasn't. The anger had disappeared as quickly as it had arrived, leaving him sapped and disgusted.

"Hormones." Bay winked at her son. She blew a kiss at him, and then she and Stanley turned around again, to lean their forearms on the porch rail.

"You guys are idiots," Miller muttered, but they weren't listening.

If Miller was certain of anything, it was that his parents' happiness was transient, and that, on Sunday, they would each go back to their separate houses, and continue their lives by themselves. He had known this since Bay had first decided on the trip. Whatever pleasure they now felt was as ephemeral as a love song.

Why couldn't they see that as well?

They were humming together, at first just dallying tunes, but then their humming coalesced and took on words: they were singing "I'm into Something Good," by Herman's Hermits. Miller knew the lyrics because his mother used to use that song as a lullaby.

On the strip of grass between Carol's house and the next, a seagull marched along proudly with a struggling red crab in its beak.

• • •

The family ate dinner that night at a seafood house on the water. Fried flounder, fried shrimp, fried clams. Corn on the cob and onion rings and shallow bowls of tartar sauce. The wind slapped them in the face and whipped their hair into their eyes. They went to the movies afterward, and then Miller walked back to Carol's and Bay and Stan strolled along the beach.

The house was quiet when Miller came in, but the lights from the street beamed through the windows along with the smell of salt and taffy and sand. Miller turned on the lights and looked at the framed pictures hanging on the wall opposite the sailfish. Bay's friend Carol—Miller recognized her from the office—was a pretty lady with shiny brown hair and lots of freckles. Her kids looked like they were maybe four or five, also freckled, and in the photos they were perched on her lap, or holding hands with Donald Duck, or stuffing their faces with birthday cake. And there was the father, handsome like the rest of them, the kind of guy who looked like he could star in a shaving-cream commercial if he wanted to. Miller gazed at the father, the mother, the children. He looked closely at all the pictures in turn, as if they could tell him how to be happy.

Later, tucked into a too-small pink-and-white bed, Miller counted the eyes of the stuffed animals watching him: four, eight, twenty, thirty-two. In the dark, he could hear the cars honk outside, and the soft moans of his parents in the bedroom down the hall, the one with the seashell wallpaper and the double bed the color of sand.

Odysseus

The next day at the beach, Bay wore a leopard-print bikini, huge red-framed sunglasses, and a wide-brimmed straw hat. She sat in a scratchy nylon beach chair and smoked cigarettes while Miller lay beside her on a towel.

"You having fun?" she asked. The sun was smack above them, the only object in the flawless sky.

"Sure," Miller said. Privately, he wished he were inside with his father, watching the ball game on television, but he didn't want his mother to feel abandoned.

"You've had that sour face on all day. It's driving me batty," Bay said, and then giggled. "This is a vacation, Joel! The beach, the sand, the waves!" She spread her arms wide. "I haven't felt so relaxed in *years*!"

"He's not coming home with us, you know," Miller said.

"Excuse me?"

Miller turned to the copy of *Rolling Stone* he'd purchased at a turnpike rest stop. He could feel his thin shoulder blades puckering and reddening in the heat.

"Repeat yourself," she said.

Miller wiped some sand out of his ear and flipped the pages of his magazine.

"I know he's not coming home with us," Bay said, after a second or two. She flicked her cigarette out toward the ocean and immediately lit another one. "Who said he was coming home with us?"

Miller tried to focus on an article about some band from Minneapolis.

"Did he say anything to you about coming home with us?" Bay asked. "Is that why you're bringing this up?"

"I'm sorry," Miller said. "I didn't mean to bring anything up."

"Did you and your father have a conversation that I don't know about?"

"There's nothing that you don't know about," Miller said. He rolled over, held the magazine up over his eyes.

"Fine," Bay said, but he could hear the pout in her voice and felt queasy. "Fine." Miller wished he could steal one of her cigarettes and smoke it right there, but he didn't have the nerve. He felt bad about that.

They sat there together as the sun proceeded across the sky, Bay periodically slathering herself with SPF 4 and humming in a high-pitched way, Miller drifting in and out of sleep. Toward three o'clock, she kicked sand on him and woke him up. "I never should have invited you," she said. "You say such horrible things to me."

Miller opened his eyes for a moment, and then closed them again, pretending to fall back asleep.

Back Home

Stan dropped Bay and Miller back at the house on Sunday afternoon, and the three of them stood awkwardly on the driveway after a few minutes of discursive agreement on what a nice weekend it was, how smooth the driving was, and what good color they'd gotten on their faces.

Stan said, "I should be getting home."

"Are you sure?" Bay asked. "Why don't you stay for supper?"

Stan looked at his watch, did a double take. "Oh, guys, I'm sorry. I've got some work to catch up on, though. I've really gotta . . . But maybe sometime this week, maybe the three of us could go out for dinner?" He looked guilty. Bay noticed it and squared her shoulders.

"Fine," she said.

"Bye," Miller said.

"Bay," Stan called, but she had already turned her back to him and was walking into the house, muttering.

"You shouldn't have done this to her, dad," Miller said. "It wasn't fair."

"What?" Stan asked. "What did I do?"

"You know. I'm not going to tell you. You know."

"She wanted me to go on vacation, I went on vacation!" Stan said. "How am I the bad guy now? Why am I always the bad guy?"

"You're not the bad guy, dad." Miller touched his father on the arm and noticed, for the first time, that he was almost Stanley's height. He stood a little straighter. "It's just that you knew what she was thinking."

"She wanted a vacation," Stan repeated, "so I gave her a vacation. I do exactly what she wants me to do and I'm still the bad guy."

Miller sighed. "She's going to make me crazy tonight, you know."

"I know," Stan said. He rubbed a beefy hand on his bright pink forehead. "I'm sorry." Then they hugged, and Stan drove back to Fort Lee.

Later that night, after take-out pizza and Diet Sprite, Bay held the cordless phone out to Miller. "I want you to call him," she said, "and see if he has a girlfriend. Ask him."

"Excuse me?" Miller said. He was watching a rerun of *Three's Company* in the living room and scratching at the wispy hair under his arm. "You want me to ask him what?"

"See if he has a girlfriend," Bay said. "I think he does. Or do you know something?"

"He doesn't have a girlfriend," Miller said. "Get out of the way—I can't see the TV."

"How do you know?" Bay asked. "Are you sure?"

"Sure I'm sure," Miller said. He changed positions on the couch so that he could maintain a clear view of the television. "He's never said a word to me about a girlfriend." He did not look his mother in the eye. He was telling the truth, but a careful version of it; when Stan hemmed and hawed on the driveway, Miller suspected he was hiding something. Until his mother said the word *girlfriend*, however, Miller had just assumed his father was hiding his enthusiasm for ditching them.

"Ask him," Bay said. She sat down next to him on the couch and handed him the phone. "Please," she said.

"If I do it, will you leave me alone?"

"I'll leave you alone," Bay said. She patted his knee. "I promise."

Miller didn't believe her, but he also knew she wouldn't rest till he placed the call, so he dialed his father's number. He let it ring once, twice, three times. He hung up when he heard his father's machine.

"He's not in."

"He said he was staying in to do some work tonight."

"I told you, he's not in."

"Try again."

"Mom."

"Leave a message."

"You leave a message," Miller said. He turned up the volume on the television. Bay sat next to him, hugging her knees to her chest like a little girl. "Jesus, mom," Miller sighed. "He's probably just out getting food."

Bay nodded tightly. She grabbed the remote control from Miller's hand and began surfing listlessly through the channels.

"Mom, I was watching something."

Bay gave him the remote, lit a cigarette, and marched out. Two hours later, on his way up to his room, Miller saw Bay sitting at the kitchen table, drawing patterns into a pile of spilled salt with the sharp end of a steak knife.

Son of Stan

The next morning, while Bay slept, Miller called his father at work and asked him. "Son," Stan sighed. "There are some things that you should know about me as a man."

"I know all about you as a man," Miller said. "Do you have a girlfriend or what?"

"I'm fifty years old. That's too old to have a girlfriend."

"You're avoiding the question."

Stan sighed again, heavily. "Do you really need to know? I mean, is this a thing that you really want to know?"

"Why did you go on vacation with mom if you have a girlfriend?"

"She's not a girlfriend," Stan said. His voice took on the same tone it had when Stan lived in the house: tired and resigned and self-pitying. Miller paced around the kitchen. He was angry.

"There are things you'll understand when you're older," Stan mumbled.

"I think that's bullshit," Miller said.

"You might be right."

There was silence, but Miller could hear his father's thick, phlegmy breathing.

"What's her name?" Miller asked finally.

"Donna McCrary," said Stan. "And I hope you'll—look, it would be nice if you gave her a chance."

But how could he? Really now. Donna McCrary. It was a name for a school nurse or a science teacher. Donna McCrary. The neighborhood busybody or the woman in charge of church picnics or the wife of the town pharmacist. Donna McCrary. Miller felt himself well with contempt at the very sound of those syllables.

One of the things that Miller had always been proud of, as far as his mother was concerned, was her name. He had never met another woman named Bay, and he thought that was terrific. Further, he loved how the name Bay brought to mind long stretches of water, seagulls, and swimming. Bay's last name, before she had married Stan, was Janovich, which was Czech and meant, roughly, "son of John." She had given Miller *Janovich* as a middle name, so Miller sometimes thought of himself as Joel son-of-John son-of-Stan Miller. He imagined that this

John was snowy-haired and wizened, maybe a blacksmith in a long-ago Czech village, with daughters and granddaughters who looked just like Bay. Miller, his head full of fruitful imaginings, was disappointed to discover, when completing a genealogy project in the fifth grade, that Bay had no specific information on John's life story. In order to finish the project, Miller was forced to rely on embellishment: the Czech village, the blacksmithing, the houseful of skinny daughters. And in the years that followed he held on to these embellishments with something close to nostalgia.

What did Donna McCrary have? Some Scottish windbag forebears full of bagpipes? Men in skirts? Tartans? What did Mc*Crary* mean, anyway? "Son of Crary"? What kind of name was Crary? And honestly, what kind of ancestor could a man named Crary possibly be?

The more Miller cogitated, the more sickened he felt, to the point where, when his father mentioned Donna the next week on the telephone, Miller was riled enough to refer to her as "that fucking Scot."

"What did you say?" Stan asked. "Fucking snot?"

"Scot," Miller corrected.

There was a long pause. "Donna's not Scottish," Stan finally said. "She's Irish-Italian."

"Whatever," Miller said.

"And be careful what you call my girlfriend, you little shit."

It was not the "little shit" that stung, but rather the word *girlfriend*. It made Miller's stomach seize. It was auspicious. Donna now had a title, an official role in his father's life.

"Son?" Stan said.

"Listen, dad, I gotta go." Miller was filled with sudden panic. "I'll see you Saturday." And he hung up the phone before his father could say anything else, grabbed his baseball glove off the kitchen table, and went running out of the house.

But it took more than an awkward phone call to dissuade

Stan. He wanted Miller, if not to like Donna, at least to meet her. Now that she was out in the open, Stan had dreams that she and Miller could become friends.

"Please, kid," he said, offering as appeasement Mets tickets, ice-cream sundaes, R-rated movies. "It'll be our little secret. Do your old man a favor." Miller couldn't stand to see his father beg, and so after a few days of negotiations he okayed the Mets tickets and agreed to meet the daughter of Crary. They made plans to have dinner Saturday at a spaghetti house in Englewood; although Miller acquiesced, he refused to be happy about it. He could never let his mother know about any of this.

"It's a new thing, son," Stan announced into the silent Cadillac on the drive to the restaurant. "She's brand-new. I mean, I met her just a few weeks before we went to the shore. Just a few dates. I didn't know it was going anywhere. I still don't know if it's going anywhere." Stan was wearing a black polo shirt and black pants. He looked, Miller thought, like a hit man.

Miller was quiet. He picked at a zit on his chin and stared out the window at the New Jersey sunset.

"Say something, would you?"

"What do you want me to say?" The sun was bright pink, a neon ball in the hazy purple-gray sky.

"Jesus, there's no reason for you to make me feel guilty," Stan said.

"I'm sorry if you feel guilty."

"You're acting like your goddamn mother."

"Leave," Miller said, "my mother out of this."

"I'm not allowed to date now? That's what this is? A divorced man and I'm not allowed to see other women? I'm being held hostage?"

Miller squeezed the zit as hard as he could and forced a thin shiny spray of pus onto the Cadillac window. He didn't say anything.

"Are you at least going to be a gentleman tonight?"

"Dad," Miller said, finally, still glaring at the sunset. "When have I ever been anything but a gentleman?"

Stan shook his head sadly as they turned into the parking lot of the restaurant. "One day you'll understand, kid."

"Yeah?" Miller said, turning to face his father, wiping his bloody chin with his wrist. "Well, maybe one day you'll understand, too."

Four Things Miller Didn't Like About Donna McCrary, Besides Her Name:

1. She never shut up about food—what was good for her, what was bad for her, what she'd eat if she could eat anything she wanted. "Why don't you just eat it, then?" Miller asked her more than once. Donna just shook her head, as though she knew truths that he, Miller, would never quite appreciate.
2. She had red hair the color of cherry Life Savers despite the fact that she was at least forty-five. Plus she wore red lipstick. Plus she wore red shoes.
3. She was sleeping with his father.
4. She was a secret.

That evening, at the restaurant in Englewood, the three ate chicken parmigiana and tortellini and drank root beer. Donna seemed nervous, which made Miller happy. Stan was talkative and ate even more than usual.

"And I hear you're a great baseball player," Donna said. She cut her food into tiny pieces and speared them precisely with her fork.

"I'm terrible," Miller said, refusing to be flattered into liking this woman.

"That's not what your father says. Your father says you're terrific."

"He kicks ass," Stan said, slurping on strings of mozzarella.

"Kicks ass!" Donna repeated, a bit giddily. "That's what your father said, that you kick ass!"

Miller felt himself start to blush, and then felt mortified that he was blushing, and then poured some hot pepper flakes onto his tortellini so that he wouldn't have to look at either Stan or Donna, and then he sneezed. He accepted Donna's offer of a handkerchief before he could remember not to.

"Bless you!" Donna said. Then she added: "Gesundheit!"

"Thanks," Miller said, and Stan beamed.

When he got home that night, Miller was happy to discover that his mother was fast asleep. Nevertheless, he suffered through his nightmare again, and woke up, for the second time that summer, in urine-soaked sheets.

Pumped

"I wish my old man had a girlfriend," Grant said. He and Miller were working out in the weight room of Stan's apartment complex, doing abs and quads, respectively. It was now late August and high school was a week away.

"Old man? What is this, 1955?" Miller said. The weight room was located in the basement of the building, small and rarely used. Miller had been spending more and more time there when he went to visit his father, partially to bulk up for his freshman year of high school, partially so that he didn't have to talk to Stan. Miller had now met Donna exactly three times and he knew that his father wanted to talk about her in a more serious fashion. Miller couldn't bear it, so he'd started bringing Grant along to Fort Lee.

"I just think it would be kind of hot," Grant said. He sat down on the edge of the abdominals machine. "My dad could use a spicy redhead in his life."

"I don't think Donna's that spicy," Miller said. "Besides, your parents are married."

"Well, if she's not spicy, what is she?"

"Oh, I don't know," Miller said. He sat down on a medicine ball and thought for a second. "I guess it's like she wants to be cool, so she brings me these stupid presents, like tapes of the Monkees she bought at a gas station for $4.99." Miller kicked at a nearby barbell scornfully. "Who the hell listens to the Monkees? Why would she buy me the Monkees?"

"Hmmrrggh," Grant growled. He had adjusted himself on the ab machine and was bending over, attached to sixty extra pounds.

"You're gonna hurt yourself."

Grant ignored him. After another set, he said, "She's probably really good in bed."

"That's gross," Miller said. It was three o'clock and Stan was out buying groceries for dinner.

"It's not that gross. You said she's never been married, right?"

"As far as I know," Miller said. He grunted, trying to sound as robust as Grant, and then he raised forty pounds above his head.

"Well." Grant whipped off his T-shirt. He stood in front of the mirror, breathing deeply and admiring his shoulder muscles. "Forty-five years old, never been married, she's probably dated around for like twenty years at least. So she's gotten a lot of practice on a lot of different guys."

"Stop it." Miller put down his weights.

"I'm just saying," Grant said, flexing his biceps and squatting. "What do you think we'll have for dinner?"

"Fish," Miller said.

"Since when do you guys eat fish? I thought you guys were like taco guys."

"Donna wants my dad to eat fish. She's worried about his heart. Anyway he's trying to lose weight or something."

Grant snorted. He put his shirt back on and wandered around the weight room, deciding what to tackle next. "Well, I guess I like fish," he said, after settling on the leg press. "My mother does some really nice things with swordfish steaks."

"You're so weird, Grant."

"No, man, you've got to taste it. She puts it out on the grill, corn on the cob, fucking great."

"I mean it. You're like the biggest queerbait I know."

"Huh," Grant said, and Miller thought he was commenting, but then he turned and saw that Grant was merely grunting from the two hundred pounds he was attempting to leg-press. School started in one week. There was no time to fuck around.

• • •

When Miller returned home to Heyward, he rushed upstairs to brush his teeth and remove any lingering scent of baked fish. Then he hurried to his room and closed the door without saying hello to his mother. Still, he knew she'd soon be searching, conducting her own sad espionage into his evening with Stan. Miller lay on his bedroom floor, reading *The Great Gatsby* with one ear cocked.

At ten o'clock she knocked and pushed the door open. "So?"

"So what?" Miller closed his book.

Bay came into his room, her eyes red and watery. She looked ten years older than she had just two months ago. She was skinnier. "What did you have for dinner?" she asked.

Trick question. "Nothing good. Could you leave? I'm trying to read."

"Tell me what you had for dinner," Bay said again. "And then I'll leave you alone."

"Why do you care?" Miller said, but then he looked up at his mother and saw how drained she was and something shifted inside him. "We had fish," he said softly.

"What kind?" Bay asked.

"I don't know," he said. "Just fish."

"Just fish," Bay said. She lay down on Miller's bed, and pulled the pillow over her head. "Just fish," she repeated, and then she began to cry.

"Mom," he said, putting down his book. "Oh, Jesus, mom, please don't. I mean it, it wasn't very good fish, it was all dried out. . . . Please stop crying." He touched his mother on the back and she started to cry harder. "Mom?" he said as gently as he could.

"Just stop lying to me, would you? Please? Would everyone just stop lying to me?" Her shoulders shook.

"I'm not lying," Miller said. "We really did have fish. I'm telling the truth."

"Oh." Bay rolled over. She took the pillow off her face. "I know you're telling the truth about that, honey," she said. "But I also know your father is seeing someone, and I wish to fucking God you'd just tell me about it instead of sneaking around here like a little goddamn rat."

"I'm not sneaking around like a rat," Miller said. He chewed on his bottom lip. Whatever sympathy he might have felt for her predicament vanished. "Could you please leave my bedroom now?"

But it became harder for Miller to look his mother in the eye, and he started answering her questions in monosyllables. Yes. No. Sure. Why? School started in six, five, four days. When she was home, Bay spent most of her time asleep on the couch. Miller stayed out of the living room. It was Labor Day. Miller ate hamburgers at Grant's. School started in three days, two, then one.

"So tomorrow's the big day," Stan said on the phone that afternoon. It was humid out, and Miller's hands felt sticky, like they'd been licked. "Let me take you out for dinner."

"Oh," Miller said. "I think mom and I were just going to get some takeout or something, actually."

Bay picked up the living room extension then. "Is that you, Stan? You're on the phone?" Shit.

"Hello, Bay," Stan said, and it occurred to Miller that his parents probably hadn't spoken to each other since the trip to the shore.

"Stanley!" Bay said. Her voice was high and brittle. "Our boy starts high school tomorrow! What do you think about that?"

"It's very nice," Stan said.

"Are you taking him out tonight?"

Miller groaned.

"I thought you and he were going to have some takeout," Stan said. "That's what you just said, isn't it, kid?"

"Takeout?" Bay asked. "Listen, I've been under the weather a little lately. A little not myself. I think it would be nice if you came and took our son out before he starts high school. I think everybody would appreciate that."

"You sure?" Stan asked. He was careful, Miller thought, about all the wrong things.

"Sure I'm sure," Bay said. "Come get him. I don't want him lying around here like a goddamn lump."

"I'm still on the phone," Miller said.

"Like a lump," Bay repeated, and hung up.

• • •

Stan picked Miller up a few hours later, and they drove north into Rockland County. Miller knew where they were headed: the barbecue joint outside Goshen. "Donna's going to be there," Stan said. Miller's appetite was dying.

She was waiting for them under the green awning outside, wearing a red flowered dress that was gathered at the waist, her red hair frizzy in the humidity. She kissed Stan on the cheek and tried to do the same to Miller, but he turned his head so she ended up bussing his ear. "Hi, handsome!" she said to him. "So, high school tomorrow, huh?"

"It's not really a big deal," Miller said.

"Oh, so nonchalant!" Donna took him by the elbow and led him into the restaurant in front of Stan.

They ate corn on the cob and barbecued chicken. Donna peeled off the skin before she let Stan have any. "So tell me," she said to Miller. "What are you going to study this year?"

Miller rolled his eyes and reached for his corn, but his father was glaring at him. "English," he said. "Geometry. Biology. U.S. history."

"All honors courses, too," Stan said, his expression softening.

"Of course," Donna said. "I remember taking biology back in high school. I just loved it. I remember we dissected cats; it was so interesting! My cat was pregnant, and so I got to look at nine little kittens, maybe the size of a finger, a small finger—no, a toe!—all curled up inside the womb. Their eyes were closed, but you could see all their kitten features just starting to shape up. The legs, the paws. The noses. It was fascinating."

"Sounds sick to me," Miller said.

"Sick!" Donna said. She seemed surprised. She put down her fork and knife. "What could be sick about discovering nature?"

"No," Miller said. "I mean, dissecting a pregnant animal. That seems sick. It's cruel."

"Oh." Donna chuckled. "It is not."

"But it is," Miller said. "Killing nine kittens!" Nine kittens!

Donna stopped laughing. Her features became narrow and sharp. "Those cats would have been born into shelters and gassed," she said.

"How do you know?" Miller asked. "Maybe someone would have wanted them for pets."

"Nobody would have wanted them," she said. "They would have been born feral, and forced to scrounge in the streets for food. Feral cats in the city. Now, that's what I call cruel. To be used as a tool for education—why, that's a privilege for those animals!" She picked up her knife and fork and began slicing up her chicken. Stan was looking at her with a mixture of admiration and surprise. Miller felt his cheeks get hot.

"You think it's better to kill a bunch of kittens for education," he said, "than it is to let them have a chance at life?"

"Life," Donna said, taking a prim sip of Coke, "is not a pretty circumstance for a bunch of stray cats."

"How do you know?" Miller said. "What makes you some sort of expert on the life of feral cats? How is it ethical to gas an animal just because"—Miller looked over at his father for help, but Stan was concentrating on his food—"just because nobody will give it a home?"

"Well, what's ethical about bringing some unwanted animals into the world to starve to death?" Donna's brown eyes were still friendly, but Miller thought that he could detect a flash of something else inside them, bright and opportunistic. "Listen," she continued, "you'll understand as you grow up, life is full of tough choices. It's best to keep a clear head about them."

While Donna was talking, Stan had eaten two whole chicken legs, with skin. There was grease on his chin.

"Well, I'm not so sure." Miller knew this was a lame response, but he was stymied. Donna's pragmatic side surprised him, although somewhere deep down he was glad she was more than sweetness and light, that his father had picked a woman with a bit of backbone. Stan furtively licked his fingertips.

When they stepped outside the restaurant, it was raining. "Phew!" Donna said, taking Stan's arm for support. "A break in the humidity!"

"I wish I had an umbrella," Stan said, and put his hand over his bald spot. Suddenly, two headlights pinned them in front of the restaurant. Miller watched, both amazed and unsurprised, as his mother got out of the car.

"Who's this?" Bay asked, her voice crackling like electricity in the air. Her hair was standing up, streaky and gray, and she was wearing shorts and that old Rutgers sweatshirt. "Who the fuck is she?" Bay asked, a little louder. So this is it, Miller thought. So here we go.

"Bay," Stan said, "this is a friend of mine. Her name is Donna."

Miller took a step away, out of the headlights' glare and into the darkness and the rain.

"When were you going to tell me, Stanley?" Bay asked. Stan and Donna were both half-protected by the restaurant's awning, but Bay was exposed and starting to soak through. Her voice crescendoed upward. "When were you going to tell me?" she cried.

"Bay," Donna said, coming forward into the rain, one hand out.

Don't touch her, Miller thought, rooted to where he stood.

"Don't touch me!" Bay shrieked.

"Bay," Stan said again, drawing Donna in. "Please, you're getting wet. Let's talk about this inside, like normal people."

"What I want to know is *when the fuck you were going to tell me*! Or were you just going to take me on vacation *and fuck me* and then disappear? Was that what you were going to do?"

"Bay," Stan said, and walked toward her. Donna was pressing herself against the restaurant wall.

"Don't touch me!" Bay shrieked again, and Miller saw that she was holding a pair of scissors. Scissors, yes, but left-handed and rubber-handled and not particularly terrifying, not even all that dangerous.

"Bay," Stan said again. He kept walking toward her. Donna seemed paralyzed. Stupid bitch, Miller thought. They're just scissors. "Bay, put those down. Come on, baby. Put them down."

"Don't call me baby," Bay said, but already her voice was softening, and she was looking at Stan with scraggly desperation.

"Bay," Stan said. "Please, honey. Come on." He was walking toward her as though he were treading a balance beam: one foot in front of the other, carefully. "Don't be silly, Bay. Come on."

She closed her eyes. He was three feet away from her, and the strands of hair that he usually combed over his bare scalp had fallen to the side of his head in sodden wisps. He advanced.

Bay sat down on the pavement of the parking lot like a paper fan folding, and the scissors fell at her side. Stan put them in his pocket.

"Okay, honey," he said. "It's okay." And he picked up his tiny ex-wife and held her in his arms.

Knives

That night, Stan stayed at the house in Heyward for the first time since he had moved out. He called Dr. Weintraub, who told him to bring her to the office in the morning. Stan hung up the phone and assessed the condition of his weak and miserable charges. For the moment, he told them, what they needed was sleep.

Miller believed this to be true. He had never felt quite as sapped before, never so in need of hours, maybe days, of simple rest. But once he was in his bed, having kissed his mother and hugged his father and turned out the lights, he found sleep impossible. Afraid he would wet the bed again—how much worse, to wet the bed while Stan was around—Miller clutched his sheets up to his neck and stared at the baseball-player pattern of his wallpaper, just barely visible in the dark. He kept imagining the headlights of his mother's car sweeping across the room. In his head, Donna McCrary said his mother's name again and again. Periodically Miller would close his eyes, telling himself he was too tired even to piss in his sleep, but then, just as he was about to drop off, he'd imagine a warm trickle down his thighs and sit up with a start, in cool dry sheets.

This is bullshit, Miller thought. It was now five in the morning, and he wasn't sure he had ever stayed up so late before. He crawled out of bed and down the stairs, past his father snoring loudly in the guest room. He half-expected to find his mother in the kitchen, but the room was empty and dark.

Miller flipped on the light and opened the refrigerator door, thinking maybe he should eat something. But the sight of stale bread and open cans of tuna made him queasy, and the smell made him feel worse. He closed the refrigerator door and thought about crackers, the hard salty kind his mother used to give him when he had a stomachache. There were probably some in the very top cupboard, and Miller kneed himself up on the counter to find out. But as he did, he noticed that he was right in front of the heavy wooden block where his mother kept the knives.

Miller slid off the counter and touched one of the heavy black handles thoughtfully. After a moment, he took the block and set it down on the kitchen table.

In the spotlight of the overhead lamp that swung over the kitchen table, the knife handles looked even more serious and professional. Each one, Miller knew, had a purpose: the slim short knife was for cutting the skins off vegetables, the long knife with the serrated edge was for bread, and the thick heavy knife, the butcher's knife, was, of course, for meat.

Miller took the butcher's knife out of the block and held the point of it gently against his wrist. He closed his eyes and tried to feel what his mother felt standing in the rain. Was it terror? Excitement? Joy? But all he could muster was a dull sense of weariness. He pressed the point of the knife against his skin, hard enough to bring up a drop of blood. He was surprised at how little it hurt. The only thing he could feel now was a sweet pulse of exhilaration. He put the knife down on the table, sat back, and watched the blood swell on his wrist.

He thought: *Now I understand. Now it all makes sense.*

He wasn't sure how long he sat there, but he slowly became aware of the sky lightening outside the room, and the birds chirping. He looked down at his wrist again; by now the blood was beginning to clot. He was suddenly aghast. What if he'd hit a vein? What if his mother saw him? What if his father did? They would freak out.

He quickly wrapped a dish towel around his wrist, and then did his best to wash off the butcher knife at the sink. There were two neat drops of blood on his Heyward Junior T-shirt. He made a mental note to wash the T-shirt, sponged the blood off the table, threw the sponge away, and put the knife block back on the counter. He was just shutting off the lights in the kitchen when he heard his father's heavy footsteps treading the upstairs hall.

"Son? That you?"

"Yeah, dad," Miller called up, keeping his arm tight against his side. He backed up into the corner of the kitchen, where maybe his father wouldn't be able to see him.

"Up early," Stan said, appearing at the kitchen door. "Quite a way to spend your last night before high school, huh?"

"What?"

"You don't want to talk about it?" Stan started plodding across the kitchen, and when he reached Miller he kissed him on the top of the head. Miller felt his wrist pulse. "That's okay. We can talk about it or not."

"Okay, dad," Miller said. He held his arm behind his back. He'd have to dig up some Band-Aids; he had no idea if there were any Band-Aids in the house. *I'm such an ass,* Miller thought to himself. *High school starts today. High school.* He had been waiting for it all summer, but somehow he had managed to forget.

PART THREE

(Concerning, Primarily, Blair Carter)

The Planet Persists

Miller's girlfriend, Lisa, and his mother, Bay, get along swimmingly, so Lisa refuses to believe Miller when he tells her that once upon a time his mother was nuts.

"What is nuts?" Lisa says. "Nuts is in the eye of the beholder. You shouldn't be so judgmental."

"My mother used to sit in the kitchen and play with the knives."

"Well"—Lisa shrugs patiently—"we all have our own ways of dealing with stress."

Lisa first met Bay during Bay's visit from San Francisco a few weeks before Miller was due to move to Park Slope. The three spent an afternoon together at Shea, and although the game was riveting (Mets 4, Giants 3; Miller hoarse from cheering), Bay and Lisa spent most of the game debating whether or not the catcher was cuter than the first baseman.

They ate dinner that night at a restaurant called Luca Bella, down the street from Miller's soon-to-be-vacated apartment. Bay and Lisa both made cooing noises over the menu and mispronounced the names of different pastas. Miller ordered a bottle of Chianti, and Bay made a face.

"You know I can't drink, sweetheart," she said. Bay had a way of saying "sweetheart" that made the word sound like mockery.

"It's for me," Miller said. "And Lisa."

"You know, if your mom can't drink, maybe we shouldn't get a bottle."

"We can easily finish a bottle," Miller said.

"I know," Lisa said, cocking her head to the left. "But maybe it's impolite . . ."

"Oh, drink if you want to, honey," Bay said. "Although it is kind of you to think of me."

"I'm not drinking," said Lisa, loudly enough for a nearby waiter to stop by their table and look concerned. "Here," she said, taking the wine list from Miller's hands and handing it to the waiter. "We won't be needing this."

"Just a scotch," said Miller. "On the rocks. Johnnie Black. For me."

Two hours later, back at Miller's apartment, they sat in an awkward configuration: Bay on the futon, Lisa on the hard-back chair in the corner, Miller standing up to brew coffee, sitting down on the floor near one woman, moving to sit next to the other. "Poor you," Lisa said. "You can't even figure out where to sit."

"Where to sit?" Miller laughed. "What are you talking about?" He was currently sitting near his mother; he shifted.

"He's always been like that," Bay said. She popped a piece of Trident in her mouth and chewed rapidly. "When his father and I got divorced—"

"Mom. Don't."

"Don't what?" Bay said. "I was telling a nice story about you."

"I don't want to talk about my father."

"I was talking about you," Bay said. "Not Stanley."

"I don't want to talk about it." Miller knew he sounded sullen. He retreated into his closet-size kitchen to check on the coffee.

"I'm sorry," Bay called out. "I should be more sensitive."

"You should be," Miller called back.

"I know," she said. "I should be, you're right. Listen, I know. I'm not the most sensitive woman in the world. People make mistakes. Don't pick on me."

When Miller came back into the living room with his coffeepot, the two women were sitting together on the futon, mid-whisper. Lisa smiled at him apologetically—*I'm sorry for siding with your mother; I just want to make a good impression*—but for a split second, a vision corralled his brain: Lisa, chain-smoking, hair standing straight up, rail-thin, running after him in the kitchen in turquoise glasses. Recoiling, his arm jerked, and the coffee splashed in its pot.

When he walked Lisa downstairs at midnight, exhausted from a whole day with his mother and two scotches on the rocks, he said, "I don't think we should move in together."

"What?" Lisa said. She pulled a stray hair away from the corner of her mouth. "You're drunk."

"I might be," Miller said. Even so, he could see his future and it looked all wrong.

"You're just freaked out because your mother's here." Under the street lamp, her eyes were beginning to fill. "You're having move-in jitters."

"We don't really know each other that well," Miller said. "What if this turns out to be a disaster?"

"Jitters," Lisa said, and although she tried to sound dismissive, her voice quavered. She pushed her glasses up her nose. "Come on, baby. We know each other just fine." She stood on her tiptoes and treated him to a soft kiss on the lips. He couldn't remember whether or not she'd ever called him "baby" before, but it sounded sort of sexy. Anyway, he was so tired.

"I'm worried," he said; that was all.

"Well, try not to be. Anyway, I'm sure enough about this for the both of us. I really am." She touched his arm quickly, then turned and hurried toward the subway before he could continue to air his doubts.

When Miller went upstairs, his mother was brewing tea, a

special chamomile blend she carried in her purse, something her doctor recommended. He could see her standing in profile in his tiny kitchen, in her neat plaid shirt, with her hair tied in a frizzy knot on her head. Her movements were fluid, her breathing calm. She was doing okay, his mother. At least he had that relief.

"Lisa is a very nice girl," Bay said, turning toward him. "You did very well for yourself with that one."

She poured her tea and sat down opposite him at the table.

"What do you mean?"

"Look," Bay said, "here's the truth. What I really hope is that she does you better than the last one. That last one could have broken my heart."

"Oh, come on, mom," Miller said, lighting a cigarette and flicking his match out the open window. "Don't start."

"You remember her?"

"I don't want to talk about it." His head was pounding. Lisa was in the subway now. Why had he said that to her? Why shouldn't he move in with her? She's crazy about him. She's a very nice girl.

"All these things you don't want to talk about. I'm just saying, remember the last one?"

"It's amazing," Miller said to his mother, "how you're always so great at saying the worst possible thing."

"Thank you very much," Bay said. "You're very kind."

Miller sighed and blew a stream of smoke out the window. Lisa was underground now, taking the 6 train to the F, while Miller sat with his mother and remembered the last one. Out the window he could see a pretty blond woman hail a cab. She had short hair and wore a blue dress, and she was slim and small and smiling. Miller knew she wasn't Blair, she couldn't be Blair, but his heart hurt anyway. It had been so long at that point, and he still couldn't figure out where he'd gone wrong.

"I'm not going to fuck it up with Lisa," he said to his mother.

"Good," said Bay. "There you go. That's what I wanted to hear."

Bong Hits

So now, today, 12:08, Saturday afternoon. Lisa is in the bathroom with a cup full of pee. Bay is in a two-bedroom flat on Filbert Street in San Francisco. And Blair Carter is gone.

Miller is looking in the mirror. He thinks he can see a gray hair.

Two years ago, a casual invitation, an empty summer weekend, a heat wave. Blair Carter's father had a beach house in the Hamptons. "You wouldn't believe it if I described it," said Rachel Jones, Grant Hershey's girlfriend. She and Blair had gone to the same prep school years before. "You've got to come check it out. We're renting a car."

"She's hot," Grant added. They were taking bong hits in his loft. "Blair's real hot."

"Plus her daddy's got a Bentley," Rachel said. She took the bong from Grant and put her mouth around the aperture. Without really wanting to, Miller paid attention to how full Rachel's lips were, and how widely she could open her mouth. She inhaled; the chamber filled with smoke; she released her manicured thumb from the carb and sucked the smoke in, smoothly. Rachel was a model and did everything with precision.

She passed the bong to Miller. "I'm serious, sweetie," she said. "You and Blair will love each other. You've got to come out with us."

"When are you leaving?"

Grant looked at his watch. "In an hour."

"Are you kidding?" Miller said. "Why didn't you bring this up sooner? It's almost midnight. And why are you getting stoned if you're driving? Jesus!" He brought the bong to his lips and inhaled sharply.

"You've got to leave at midnight," Rachel explained. She put her thin brown hand on Miller's leg. "Beat the Friday traffic."

"I don't have any of my shit with me."

"What do you need?" Grant asked. "A bathing suit? You can borrow one of mine."

"You wear Speedos, you prick."

"Come on," Rachel said. She ran her hand up and down Miller's leg. "It'll be so much fun. You'll love it out there. Have you ever been?"

Miller shrugged. He was getting gooseflesh where Rachel touched him.

"I have a bathing suit that's *not* a Speedo," Grant said. He picked up the bong and stared down into the chamber. "I'm almost certain. It's green."

"Come on, Miller," Rachel said drowsily. She leaned back against Grant. "It'll be soooo fun."

"No, it's blue."

"What is?"

"My bathing suit."

"Okay," Miller said, laughing. "But does Blair know I'm coming? Does she know to expect me?"

"Of course!" Rachel said. "We told her all about you, sweetie. And she couldn't be more delighted."

A Man Who Learns

That summer night, Miller was living in New York City. He was there because he had followed a girl. After so many years living with his mother, he'd become good at being around women, knew to compliment the qualities they felt insecure about, knew to listen to them without interrupting. He'd met a girl his senior year at Brown—a girl, he thought, not a woman—twenty-one years old with a pink streak in her hair, a tattoo of a butterfly around her navel, that sort of thing. Stan professed not to like her, but Miller could tell he thought she was something. Her name was Debra and she wanted to act.

Even though he had grown up a mere six miles from the big city, when Miller was twenty-two, New York was still fairly foreign to him. His parents were both born and raised in New Jersey, and to them, driving across the Hudson was as daunting as swimming the English Channel. Sure, they went in occasionally: a Broadway show once a year with Bay's parents, a fancy meal for fancy occasions, stiffened up in suits and shoes they hadn't worn in months. But in general, his parents thought New York was Too Loud, Too Dangerous, Too Expensive; they liked it well enough in the suburbs where the stores closed early and everyone had a car. Stan's only exception was Shea Stadium, and to get there you never even had to leave the highway. This Debra of Miller's had been born and raised in Brooklyn, and to Miller that fact was as exotic as the silver stud in her labia.

He found a job. It was 1996 and not such a hard thing to do. There was a website called BigFunCity, and they sent Miller to the symphony twice a month, and to restaurants, and periodically to auctions of such things as African masks or a dead eccentric's ladybug collection. He wrote reviews of these occasions, mustering some humor about events—like the ladybug auction—that were mostly just dusty and bizarre. He longed to work at BigFunCity long enough to become the literary editor. Debra worked on Miller's wardrobe, and he started wearing T-shirts that were as old as he was and tight, tattered pants.

The website couldn't pay very much—Grant referred to Miller's paycheck as "fucking toilet paper"—but nonetheless he rented an apartment on Steinway Street, in Queens. It was a basement apartment, but there was a little kitchen and a big bathroom and access to a tiny plot in the back, full of sooty city squirrels, that the landlady called a "garden."

Bay had long since moved to San Francisco. When Miller phoned her to tell her about his apartment, she said, "Steinway! Like the piano! Very classy, honey." Miller knew what his mother envisioned: high city ceilings and views of the Empire State Building, shiny wooden floors and a doorman with a firm navy cap. Instead he had cracked linoleum and a futon on the floor, and the whole of it was lit by a single, unshaded lightbulb, but the apartment was his own and it seemed exactly right. He put a shoebox full of his father's baseball cards in the closet and a picture of Bay on the wall, and let piles of books and laundry collect around him like friendly roommates.

Debra lived nearby. Most nights during their first three months in New York, she would show up with a grease-stained bag of food from one of the Steinway Street vendors. Miller's neighborhood was traditionally Greek, but it also hosted Pakistani, Egyptian, Thai, and Afghan immigrants; every night he and Debra invited strange smells and potential stomach distress into the apartment via the takeout of these and other nations. They were particularly fond of the spicy eggplant from the Kurdish joint on Broadway.

When Debra showed up one night in August with a bag from regular old KFC, Miller recognized trouble.

"So I've been thinking about Los Angeles," she said, chewing on a pasty fist-sized biscuit.

Los Angeles? Miller thought. No fucking way. "What about New York? Didn't we just get here?"

"There's nothing in theater anymore. Nothing! If I want to be an actress, I've got to stop dicking around. Mill, it's L.A. or bust."

Debra had been auditioning every day and had yet to be cast for anything; while publicly Miller told her it was just a matter of time, the truth was he had seen her version of Maggie in an off-off-Broadway production of *Cat on a Hot Tin Roof*. He feared perhaps it was more a matter of talent.

"I like it here," Miller said. He poked at his chicken. It was true; he did like New York, found himself liking it more every day. Even the city's noises had started to seem companionable: the fire engine's passionate wail, the percussive rumble of the trains. The bookstores were well stocked and most of the bars were welcoming. And although Miller liked Debra, too, he knew there were limits to how much he would like her. His fondness for New York, however, seemed infinite. "I don't want to go to L.A."

"Yeah," Debra said. "I thought you might say that. I understand." She lay back on the futon like an invitation, long brown hair and big brown eyes and a waist so skinny she bought her jeans in the kids' section. Miller climbed on top of her and then they fell asleep; eight days later she was gone.

He missed her, but not in a debilitating way. He was busy with his job, going to the office and the auctions. Plus he was always meeting new people, frequently through Grant, who had a job as an investment banker at a big midtown firm. Grant worked seventy hours a week, but when he wasn't working he threw parties at bars in Tribeca or Soho. He squired different ladies to these parties, tall and thin as lampposts, with cigarettes hanging from their lips and wire bracelets clamped around their upper arms. Miller fell in love with most of these women and sometimes would sit in a corner, sip on a Corona, and wish Debra were still around. But by February he stopped getting phone calls from her, and by March he didn't think about her much at all.

This time Grant fixed Miller's wardrobe. Out went Debra's torn pants and artfully overwashed T-shirts; in came slim gray trousers and Grant's own gently preworn cashmere sweaters. I look like Eurotrash, Miller complained, but he also noticed that his success with the friends of Grant's girlfriends picked up, which was cheering.

In 1999 Grant met a girl named Rachel. She was tall and

brown and British, and she was so beautiful that Miller sometimes got a headache looking at her. She had a friend named Blair Carter. She thought Miller might like her.

This all happened two years ago.

First Things

So that night they finished their bong hits and took off for Bridgehampton a little after twelve. Four hours later, in the blue-black darkness, Miller could not determine the size of the house at which they arrived or the make of the car in the driveway. They had driven east on the Long Island Expressway for an hour and a half, and soon after had become very lost off Route 27. They had argued with each other and then grown silent—when Rachel finally found the house ("I told you it was here, you bungholes"), they felt more exhaustion than relief.

The woman who opened the door was not pleased. She wore a T-shirt and sweatpants and her blond hair was flat against one side of her head. Her eyes were at half-mast; her skin was blotchy. They had been ringing the doorbell for at least ten minutes.

"I cannot believe," the woman said, "what jerks you guys are. It's four in the morning."

"Traffic," Rachel said. "Sweetie, I'm so sorry."

The woman nodded sleepily at the apology and stepped aside to let them in, first Rachel, then Grant, then Miller.

"Who are you?" she asked him as he walked in. Her breath smelled like mouthwash.

"I'm Miller. I'm a friend of Grant's. I thought you knew I—"

"Miller," she said. "A friend of Grant's." She looked at him for a moment, assessing. Her eyes opened all the way. They were shockingly blue. Finally she seemed to come to a conclusion. "Well, Miller, Anita only made up one of the guest rooms. Unexpected guests," she said, turning away from him, "have to sleep on the couch."

Miller, tired and foggy from the marijuana, told her that that would be just fine.

In a White Room

The couch was white. The floor was white. The ceilings, peaking sharply two stories above him, were white. The walls, which formed a hexagon overlooking a bay, were mostly glass, but the parts that were not glass were white. There was a table in a corner made of very pale wood, which, in turn, supported a massive white vase containing a massive profusion of flowers. Which were, to a petal, white.

Miller woke up at six thirty in the morning wincing from the glare.

"Shit," someone said. "I forgot to do this last night." Miller sat up on the couch and saw Blair, her eyes wide and bright, her hair hidden under a baseball cap. "I'm really sorry," she said. "It's just that you guys got here so late. I was too tired to put sheets on one of the guest beds, and they're not usually made up for random visitors. . . ." She was standing in the corner of the room wearing a nylon tracksuit in a riot of pink and blue. She pressed a button on the wall, and like magic the windows turned cloudy, then opaque. The room was once again dark. "Are you comfortable?" she asked him.

"Yes," Miller said. "Thank you. And I'm sorry to intrude. Rachel told me that she'd asked you—"

"She didn't," Blair said. "Rachel lies a lot." They both were quiet for a minute. Finally, Blair said, "I'm going for a run. At seven thirty there will be coffee in the kitchen. It's down the hall; you'll see it." Then she disappeared, and the room was once again monochrome. Miller closed his eyes and fell back asleep.

Look, what could he have known back then? How could he have known? Sure, Blair seemed cute, but not so much cuter than the other women Grant had produced for Miller's quietly enthralled observation. It had been several seasons since Debra Fox had disappeared for seasonless Los Angeles, and in that time Miller had met many women and sometimes, if he was lucky, got taken home like a party favor. But he knew who he was, the twenty-seven-year-old he'd become. Too tall, too skinny, bumpy-nosed and nearsighted. Halfway between klutzy and adorable, trying to lean as far as he could toward adorable but sometimes snorting during a laugh or lighting the wrong end of a cigarette and ending up fucked. But he was growing used to himself. He knew his own limitations.

His mother called periodically to check in; his father, alone in Fort Lee—Donna McCrary had long since departed—invited him over for dinner once a month. They both gave Miller their opinions: he was too disorganized, too messy, too lax. Why didn't he have a better job, Bay wanted to know, when she discovered that Steinway Street was not exactly Fifth Avenue. Didn't he have an Ivy League education? Weren't his sneakers supposed to be tapping down gold-paved streets? What's to be proud of? I want, Bay announced, to be proud!

Miller's father, in his phlegmatic way, looked at Miller's circumstances less hysterically but with more disdain. He was just a kid, he didn't know what life would bring, but no harm was ever done in getting an MBA and meeting a nice girl. Miller found easy protests: But you got an MBA, dad! You met a nice girl! And is your life what you thought it would be? A rented condo and a half-empty bed?

This isn't about me, kid. It's about you.

Frankly, at twenty-seven Miller was lucky and lucky enough to know it: healthy and financially liquid. He had a best friend, he got laid once in a while, and now he was in the Hamptons, at a stranger's summer castle, perfectly free. And as he drifted in and out of cloudy white sleep, Miller could hear swans honking in the bay.

Later, thinking about the last half hour of his life before he began to love Blair Carter, Miller would assign that couch and his drifting sleep a sincerely missed innocence. Oh, if only I'd known, he'd think to himself. . . . If only I had known, I would have gotten up and run across the whole of Long Island until I was back in my basement in Queens. Fuck the castle. Fuck the bay. I would have put on my sneakers, and if I couldn't find my sneakers I would have run barefoot, and if I couldn't run barefoot then I would have hopped, or bicycled, or pogo-sticked.

Botulism

At a quarter to eight, Miller was awake again, lured off the couch by the coffee smell, which he followed blindly down a long tile-floored hall to the kitchen. Lining the hall was a series of framed photographs of a toddler with robin's-egg eyes—Blair, two or three—and short blond curls tangling around her face. On the opposite wall was a giant print of a lean graying man with his arm around an adolescent Blair. They were standing on a winter beach, silvery water behind them and dark clouds above. Even though the man was barefoot, his chinos rolled up under his knees, he looked dignified, protective, rich. Miller looked down at his own jeans and wondered if he could pull off the barefoot beachfront look.

In the middle of the kitchen there were four clay mugs on a large marble island, and a note: GOOD MORNING!

"Morning," Blair Carter said. She was on a stool at the marble island, shiny from her run. "It's going to be a mess of a day," she said. "Serious downpour coming later."

"How can you tell?" Miller asked. The kitchen's north wall looked out on the bay and a vast blue sheet of sky. Nothing ominous.

"There are clouds to the north. Plus the stillness outside," Blair said. "Everything's so still." She had poured herself some orange juice in a big glass tumbler; it looked a little greenish around the edges. Miller stood and drank his coffee, a bit at a loss. She held the tumbler up to the light above them and looked at it critically.

"This look greenish to you?" she asked him.

"A little."

"Think it's botulism?" she asked.

"Is botulism green?"

She shrugged and looked around. "I could go down to the farmers' market," she said. "I could get some new juice." Miller sat down on the stool on the other side of the big marble island. He wished he could see what she looked like without that stupid baseball cap hiding her hair. "Of course," Blair continued, "it would be pointless to buy orange juice at the farmers' market, considering oranges are not native to Long Island, and I could squeeze my own damn juice from whatever I buy at King Kullen. Is fresh-squeezed important to you, Miller?" she asked.

"Not especially," he said. "I don't think about it much."

"Fresh ground coffee?" she asked.

"I drink Maxwell House."

"Organic produce?"

"I haven't bought a vegetable in years," he said. He knew he was being contrary.

She looked at Miller like he was from a country she'd never visited. "Do you eat fast food?" she asked him.

"What, like McDonald's?" he said. "Sometimes."

"Hmmm." She adjusted her cap and continued to regard him. He couldn't tell if she was displeased but also intrigued, or just displeased. He suddenly felt acutely aware of his hair, and tried to pat it down. She smiled. "I guess I shouldn't tell you the kind of shit you can find in a McDonald's hamburger. What I mean is fecal matter."

"Don't tell me."

"It's true," she said. She pushed her orange juice glass around on the marble island. "They've done tests."

"It's one of those things I'm just as happy not knowing."

"You should take care of yourself," she said. "Or you should find someone else to take care of you." She smiled again. Once more Miller tried to pat down his hair, but then he realized how uncool he looked so he stopped. "I'm going to the market," she said. "Wanna come?"

He had never been in a Bentley before, but the interior was much as he suspected it would be—shiny chrome and burled wood and pillow-soft leather seats. Blair pressed a button, and the top folded down behind them with a slow, stately creak. When she turned the key, the car hummed into gear. She pressed another button, and suddenly they were listening to Fleetwood Mac.

"Soft rock," she said, crossing her eyes at Miller. "My father can't get enough."

They backed all the way down the half-mile path that fronted the house. At Mecox Lane, Blair executed a sloppy three-point turn that momentarily placed them on the wrong side of the road. "I am," she said to Miller over the wind, "an impressively poor driver." Then she switched lanes and pressed down on the gas. They were carried off toward Route 27 with the morning sun shining on their heads and the bay spreading out beside them.

Four Things to Notice in a Grocery Store, Especially While in the Company of a Fine-Looking Woman:

1. In the right light, fruit is beautiful. Firm fuzzy peaches and pink and green mangoes, spiky yellow pineapples, sunny purple plums. Blair walked the fruit aisles with an almost regal air of approval, inhaling the ripe spiciness of a persimmon, giving a nectarine an indecent squeeze.
2. Meat is less beautiful. The luster of a bloody hunk of lamb loin cannot help but be diminished when glared at by a cute blonde in a tight shirt.

3. There are too many flavors of ice cream. After a certain amount of back-and-forth, Blair settled on French vanilla. "This will be good for later," she said. "I'll bake a pie." Miller bit his lip to keep from smiling too wide.
4. Men will look. Frat boys in the beer aisle, fathers with kids swinging their legs in the cart, old men buying cottage cheese, teenagers buying Doritos—they all will look at the beautiful girl, and when they see she's with you, they will let out sullen sighs and shake their heads.

Miller followed Blair Carter around King Kullen the way Harry follows him through the apartment when he needs to be fed. He brushed her arm near the deli counter. Shit, he thought. He hadn't even known her for a day yet, and already, like a jerk, he was falling in love.

Cooking Lesson

Weatherwise, and against Blair's dire predictions, the day progressed as it had started: sunny, breezy, warm. "She's cute, right?" Grant said. It was around four in the afternoon and he was sitting with Miller by the pool, drinking a Negra Modelo. He was wearing a red Speedo and an elaborate beaded bracelet around each wrist.

"Blair?" Miller asked, hiding his eyes from the sun with a copy of *Fear and Loathing in Las Vegas*. "I guess so, if you like vegetarians."

Grant snickered and stole a Camel from Miller's pack. He lit it with an exaggerated motion, flipping up the Zippo against his thigh. "Didn't you read that shit in high school like everyone else?" he said.

Grant was such a bully. Miller sighed and put the book down. "What do you know about her?"

"Kind of a loner. Cute but weird," Grant said, lowering his voice. "She doesn't have too many friends besides Rachel, and even she and Rachel aren't that close. But her major problem is she's got this daddy thing. Nobody competes with Reynold."

"Well, didn't you say the man was like an ambassador or something?" Miller asked.

"Years ago. When Blair was a kid. Now he sits around all day and counts his money."

"Doesn't sound too bad to me."

"And Blair is his secretary. Doesn't make a move without her."

"So?"

"Are you listening to me? She dropped out of college to take care of her father."

"So she's a devoted daughter," Miller said.

Grant snickered again. "Sometimes I wonder if they've ever gotten it on," he said, blowing smoke rings. "Reynold and Blair."

"Don't be an idiot," Miller said.

"It's possible." Grant exhaled. "Her mother's been dead for nineteen years. Blair was like his ambassadress—"

"Is *ambassadress* a word?"

"You know what I mean. Hosted dinners with him. Was his date to every single diplomatic function. And isn't it weird how Reynold never remarried?"

"You met the guy?"

"*Nobody's* met the guy," Grant said, and waggled his eyebrows suggestively. "Not even Rachel. There's just that one picture of him in the hall."

"That doesn't prove anything."

"Doesn't it?" Grant said. Miller lit his own cigarette and thought about it—and then determined that, no, it didn't prove anything at all.

Rachel emerged from the house wrapped in a bikini top and a sarong the same color as Grant's Speedo. She was carrying a glass of wine and a bowl of olives. "Ooh!" she said, seating herself at the end of Grant's deck chair. "Sunny!" She put the bowl and the glass down on the deck and proceeded to untie her bikini top and throw it into the pool. "I'll get a tan."

"Hi there," Grant said, and rubbed her bare back with his toe.

"Hi there," she said, and leaned back on him, so that she was lying on his legs and her breasts were pointed up at the sky.

"Maybe I'll head inside."

"Oh, Miller," Rachel said. "Don't be a prude. They're just breasts. You've seen breasts before, right?"

"Not yours," Grant murmured. He took a long drag on his cigarette.

"Well, what's the difference?" She giggled. "Knockers are knockers."

"But yours are the best," Grant said. He ran his foot up and down Rachel's outer thigh. "They don't make them better than yours."

Rachel giggled again. Miller went inside. The kitchen was cool and dim and a relief.

"They're being repulsive?" Blair asked. Her voice surprised him. She was standing at the marble island, chopping the tomatoes they had bought that morning. She had changed out of her running gear and was now wearing a white T-shirt and white jeans. He stood next to her.

"Not repulsive, just affectionate," Miller said. "But maybe it's a little tough to take."

He watched her cut the tomatoes, her hands moving deftly. The cubes she produced were tiny and perfect. Miller thought about Bay, who usually made dinner by pouring things out of cans. He wondered if Blair made dinner for her father.

"Where'd you learn to cook?"

"All over the place," Blair said. "I grew up in Austria, but we had a French woman in charge of the kitchen and she taught me some of the basics—you know, roasted chicken and tomato soup and the right way to make a salad."

"What's the right way to make a salad?" Miller asked. She was now chopping cucumbers into the same perfect dice.

Blair smiled. She turned and grabbed a bulb of garlic from a basket. "I'll show you," she said. "Hand me one of those wooden bowls from that shelf." Miller did, and then watched as Blair crushed two cloves of garlic into the bowl's bottom with a fork. Then she poured in some olive oil, a long syrupy stream of it, and salted and peppered the slick at the bottom of the bowl. She sprinkled in a few drops of vinegar, grabbed a head of lettuce out of a colander in the sink, and began tearing up the lettuce into the bowl. Finally, she mixed the whole thing up with her hands.

"That's it?" Miller asked.

"*Salade*," Blair said, wiping her hands on a dishrag. She took a piece of lettuce out of the bowl and munched. "You should try some."

"Fork?"

"Please," she said. "Use your fingers."

So Miller stuck his fingers into the salad bowl. A prickly warmth spread through his hands as he touched the lettuce that Blair had touched. He put a piece in his mouth: it was garlicky and salty and sweet.

"Good?" she asked him.

"Very," Miller said.

Blair pushed a piece of hair behind her ear and turned away. It seemed to Miller that perhaps she was starting to blush. He looked down at his fingers so as not to embarrass her further, if indeed he had been embarrassing her at all. Maybe it was Miller who was starting to blush? He put a hand to a cheek, which felt a bit warm.

Wonderland

Blair's father kept a dinghy moored to a weathered dock on Mecox Bay, an excellent perch from which to view the sunset.

A little before eight that evening, Miller and Rachel followed Blair through the reeds behind her house, Miller carrying a bottle of wine, Rachel carrying the glasses. When they reached the dock, the sun had begun to dip below the horizon, bright pink and swollen.

"I should have woken Grant up," Rachel said. "He'd love this." Grant had fallen asleep inside the house, in front of *SportsCenter*.

"No," Blair said. "The boat can just about handle three people. Four would sink it."

Across the narrow bay, grand houses blazed with light. Some were old-fashioned and stately, with columns and porticoes and marble statues of naked women facing the water. Others took their cues from modern art museums: stone and wood structures with roofs that slanted at roller-coaster angles and glass wings jutting toward the bay.

"Look at that one," Rachel said. "It glows." Diagonally across the bay stood a low stone house whose roofline was rimmed with blue neon.

"Maybe it's an art installation. People here consider themselves experts on fine arts," Blair said. "People here consider themselves experts on everything."

The three eased themselves into the dinghy and Blair poured wine into their glasses. The boat rocked gently as the sun continued its descent. Ducks poked their heads into the reeds that lined the shore, and minnows darted just beneath the water's surface.

"This must have been a wonderland when you were a kid," Miller said.

"It was," Blair said. "It still is." In the air a dragonfly buzzed. "It's nice to come out here, especially in the winter, when it's empty and quiet. It doesn't get as cold out here as it does in the city, and all the birds come back from Canada and take over the woods and the ponds."

"So is this where you disappear to?" Rachel said. "You know, half the time when I try to find you it's impossible. I call you in the city, I try you on your cell phone, you're nowhere to be found. It's a miracle I found you here last night. The incredible disappearing woman."

Blair shrugged. "The incredible disappearing woman? Sometimes I just don't hear the phone."

"How could you not hear the phone for months at a time?"

"It happens to me too." Miller rushed to Blair's defense. "I'll just tune out, sometimes for entire days. I'll be reading or working and the phone rings and I won't hear it."

"That's crazy," said Rachel. She was a woman who wouldn't dream of being out of contact, for a day or for an hour. Even now she had her cell phone tucked into her pocket. "That's almost passive-aggressive."

Miller and Blair both shrugged.

"There could be an emergency." Rachel sat forward. "What if somebody really needs you?"

"Come on, Rachel," Blair said, her voice gentle. "Nobody needs me that badly."

Miller looked at Blair longingly. She was wearing a navy blue sweater and her white jeans, her feet bare and resting in a puddle on the dinghy's floor. "Somebody must need you that badly," Miller said. "There's got to be someone."

"Nope." Blair took a sip of her wine. She splashed her toes in the puddle at the boat's bottom, and then smiled up at Miller. "There's nobody at all. Of course, that's the way I like it."

"What rubbish," Rachel said. "What about your father?"

But Blair just continued to smile at Miller, like an offer, or a dare.

Tourism

Before piling back into the car toward Manhattan, Miller asked Blair if she'd ever had Kurdish takeout. He acted dismayed when she said she hadn't. "Kurdish?" she said in disbelief.

"Oh, you really should." So: plans, cunningly arrived at. He coughed as he asked her to come by for dinner. Grant and Rachel pretended not to hear the machinations. Blair looked down, looked up, agreed.

And came over the next Thursday. Miller spent the two hours before her arrival checking over his apartment and seeing things he'd never noticed before: knee-high chips in the gray paint on the walls, a mud-colored stain on the beige carpet, near the Salvation Army couch, and a funky, sweaty smell emanating from the futon. He changed the futon's sheets, cursed, wondered if Dial-A-Mattress could guarantee delivery in an hour, cursed again when he found that they could not. He tried to soak up the mud-colored stain with some old T-shirts dipped in Lysol. He stared fixedly at the chips in the paint and considered what on earth could have been their cause.

He bought a six-pack of Negra Modelo. He showered and tried to paste down his hair into something resembling neatness. He tried on one of Grant's old button-down shirts, took it off, and put it back on. He wore clean jeans. He stayed barefoot, because Debra Fox once told him that he had very attractive feet.

Blair arrived five minutes early.

"So this is where you live." She kissed him on the cheek. She was prettier than he had remembered, and smaller, barely five three, slim and strong like a cord of wood. Her blond hair, free of that horrible cap, swept gently behind her ears. She was wearing a black cotton dress.

"This is where I live." Miller stepped back to let her in. "Ever been to Queens before?"

"The airports." She walked around his apartment, seemed to inspect it the way Miller had. "And the U.S. Open."

"Well, welcome." Miller was proud to introduce her to someplace she hadn't been before. Queens, he felt, was a different kind of wonderland, one everybody should try at least once.

"Glad to be here," Blair said. "Are we really eating Kurdish?"

"Here's the menu." Miller passed her a xeroxed menu from a kitchen drawer. They both looked at it together in what Miller hoped was companionable silence, pondering sheikh babani and kubay sawar. "That's a good one," Miller said, pointing to the babani. "It's eggplant."

They got straight to it, rather than mumble through forced conversation, ordering the babani, plus spicy spinach and cracked-wheat dumplings and bread. "I brought beer." Blair pulled a six-pack of Corona out of her knapsack. "I'll put it in the fridge. Oh, you already have Negra Modelo! Well, okay. No such thing as too much beer."

"I can't believe you haven't been to Queens for anything but the airport," Miller said to Blair's back, watching her ass as she leaned into the refrigerator.

"Not a lot of time spent exploring, I'm afraid." She closed the refrigerator door with her hip, holding a Corona in each hand. "I spend most of my time in the city helping my father. He travels so much, and he doesn't trust anyone else to do his personal accounts."

"So you're like his secretary?"

Blair looked bemused. "Sort of."

Miller flashed back to Grant's lewd guesses about Blair and her father. "Isn't there anything else you'd rather be doing?" he asked.

"Sometimes," Blair said, "I think it might be nice to try my hand at something new. I used to want to be a high school history teacher. But, I don't know, my father's just really dependent on me, and it would be hard to let him down. Besides, the world has enough history teachers."

"The world doesn't have enough good history teachers."

Blair patted Miller on the hand. "I have no idea whether or not I'd be any good."

"Let's go outside," Miller said.

Sitting on the stoop, drinking their beers, their legs touched intentionally but casually. Miller took a deep breath and allowed himself to enjoy her body's warmth, not give in to nerves and pull away. He wondered if she had done this before with other boys, sat on a stoop drinking beer. He supposed not. Her other dates were probably four-star-hotel types, or guys who could whip up an exotic and difficult dinner while chatting to her in French. Maybe, instead of just getting Kurdish delivered, Blair's previous dates had flown her to Kurdistan for an authentic food experience. But he was not going to dwell on her previous boyfriends. Miller reached for a cigarette.

Blair sat regally, her bare legs crossed at the ankles, her posture straight. Her legs and ankles were slim, but the calf muscles bulged. Must be all the running, Miller thought. A few strands of her hair blew around her face. He wanted to reach out and tuck the hair back behind her ear, but didn't dare.

They stayed quiet, just watched the traffic on Steinway, kids with boom boxes and men in groups smoking and old ladies yelling at each other in Spanish and Greek. The evening was warm and the sky full of fading summer light.

"I like it here," Blair said. "It's a shame all those highways sweep over Queens. Drive all the way out to Long Island and you have no idea what you're missing."

"Well, the people headed for Long Island probably wouldn't miss Queens even if they knew what was here." Down the street, a man in grimy clothes pulled aluminum cans from a trash bin. "It's sort of an acquired taste."

Blair nodded and scratched at her delicate ankle. The man in grimy clothes looked up from his trash bin and stared at her.

"Frank Lloyd Wright said that New York is the biggest mouth in the world," Miller said. "I always liked that."

"What do you think he meant, exactly?"

Miller spied the delivery guy pedaling up the street, bearing their Kurdish dinner in his bicycle basket. "Time to eat."

Nomenclature

He set up a picnic on the floor by the kitchen, spreading out a sheet on the carpet to cover up its stain. There were plastic plates and paper towels and the flimsy cutlery that came with the food. Blair opened up the containers, and the basement air filled with the smells of garlic and pepper and onions.

"It's good, right?" he asked her.

"Mmmdelicious," she said.

"There's other great food to try," he enthused. "Moroccan and Thai, and there's a Brazilian place just down the street—"

"Can I ask you a question?" Blair asked.

"Anything."

"Do they always call you by your last name?"

"My last name?"

"Miller is your last name, right?"

"Yeah." He nodded. "My first name's Joel, but nobody really calls me that except sometimes my mother."

"How come?"

"Baseball." He put down his fork and leaned back on his hands. "In the third grade, my dad coached my baseball team, and he called us all by our last names. We called him Coach."

"Wouldn't it have been easier for him to call you Joel?" she asked. "Wasn't that what he was used to calling you?"

"Nah," Miller said. He twisted open another beer and took a sip, watched her scoop up spicy spinach with a sheet of doughy bread. She really was so pretty. "My father's always called me 'son,' " he said. "I'm not sure why. When I played third base he called me Miller, just like he called all the other kids by their last names."

"You played third base?"

"Only when I was little. In junior high," he said, "I played right field. It's sort of a power hitter's position."

Blair looked at him. She had a tiny piece of spinach between her teeth. "Could I call you Joel?" she asked. Her dress was cut low so that her collarbone and her neck were wholly exposed.

"Why?" Miller asked.

"It's a nice name," she said. "It's your name."

"Everybody calls me Miller," he said.

"So you said." She picked up her bread, looked at it for a moment, and then popped it in her mouth. "Why don't you make eye contact when you talk, Joel? You seem shifty."

"What? I make eye contact."

"Not always."

"That's a new one. Nobody's ever accused me of being shifty before. Really."

"I didn't say you *are* shifty," Blair said. "I just said you *seem* shifty. When you're not looking at me."

"I don't know what you're talking about. I'm looking at you right now."

"Are you?" Blair asked, and Miller wondered what she was getting at.

"Of course."

Miller studied the three gold studs, tiny, like pinpoints, in each of Blair's ears. He studied her neat white teeth with the spinach caught between them, and the faint line of a scar running from below her lip down to her chin. "Where'd you get that scar?" he asked.

"Fell off a swing," she said. "When I was three. The nanny was smoking a cigarette and couldn't catch me in time." She touched it gently. "What about you?"

"Nothing remarkable," he said. "My knee's torn up from falling when I was a kid. And I have this one." Miller pushed up his sleeve so she could have a better look.

"What's that from?" she asked, scooting over and peering down at the raised pink dot on the inside of his wrist.

"I was playing with a knife," Miller said. "The summer before high school. Kind of got carried away."

"Playing with a knife?" Blair said. She placed a perfect finger on his scar. Miller decided that he would tell her the story some other time. She looked up at him. He touched her shoulder. When they kissed, all garlicky spinach and hot sauce, Miller felt his heart take off and fly.

Our Familiars

She called two days later, Saturday, early afternoon. As she had said she might. Miller had been playing a game with himself: timing the intervals between thoughts of Blair Carter by closing his eyes, forcing himself to drift, and then checking in with the big yellow-faced alarm clock next to his bed. He was still in bed, mostly naked, except for one fleecy blue sock on his left foot. He had lazily jerked off almost an hour before. So far, the longest he had gone without thinking about Blair was twelve minutes. He lit a cigarette. She called. 1:06.

"Let's take a walk," she said without preamble. It was as though she knew he had been thinking, hoping, half-expecting, praying, and that she had been waiting for him to boil over.

"Yes," he said. "Where?"

"Can you meet me in Washington Square Park? Under the arch? In an hour?"

Can I be on the moon in an hour?

"No problem," Miller said.

After she hung up, Miller rolled over but did not get out of bed. He was suddenly half-erect. He closed his eyes.

In the forty-eight hours since he'd last seen Blair, Miller had received the following intelligence over early-evening drinks with Rachel: Blair was born in Vienna, Austria, in February; she was a Pisces ("placid, patient, a bit of a loner—darling, don't you know your zodiac?"). Her last real boyfriend moved to Tokyo three years ago, and since then she'd dated sporadically, mostly bankers and lawyers, but nobody in particular. ("What, the boyfriend? Well, rather wealthy, yes, and good-looking in a sort of simple Connecticut way. Blondish, if I remember correctly. Handy on the squash court. But he was certainly shorter than you are, Miller, so simmer down.")

According to Rachel, there was not much else to report. Blair lived with her father in nine rooms on Park Avenue but visited the Hamptons often, and in the springtime she traveled to Europe. She had been an indifferent student and dropped out of Bennington four semesters in, but to the best of Rachel's knowledge her father didn't seem to mind that decision. Rachel had no idea Blair harbored a desire to become a high school history teacher. In truth, she'd always found Blair refreshingly unacademic.

After another Bloody Mary, Rachel admitted that back in high school several classmates—herself included—had assumed that Blair was a lesbian. This assumption was not due to any particular fondness Blair demonstrated toward her Miss Porter's School fellows (in fact, she had always seemed a bit detached from them, remote even), but rather because of her utter disinterest in boys, leg-shaving, gossip. Several years later, a collective sense of agreeable surprise developed among these classmates when the blondish gentleman from Connecticut began squiring Blair to the few social events she attended: fund-raisers, the occasional cocktail party.

"Miller," Rachel said, poking the celery stick from her Bloody Mary in his direction. "As I'm sure you've determined,

Blair Carter is in no way a lesbian. So please get that slimy little look off your face."

"What do you mean, slimy?" Miller had blushed.

Enough remembering! Into the shower, out of the shower, deodorant, hair, wardrobe. It was a pleasant summer Saturday. This called for a green polo shirt with a tiny knit skull where other shirts might sport an alligator (subversive, offbeat, a gift from Debra), and dirty-ish khakis, scuffed at the bottoms, a little loose, phew. Miller gelled his hair into an appropriate arrangement of swirls and spikes and then messed up the arrangement so as not to look too deliberate. He was off.

Blair was under the arch when he arrived. He was three minutes early, which meant that at minimum she was four. She seemed to be slightly better than punctual. He remembered how late they'd all been to the Hamptons, and shivered.

"Hello," she said.

"Hello."

And now he wasn't quite sure what the appropriate physical greeting was—sure, they'd spent an extremely satisfactory forty-five minutes making out on his floor, during which his hands had crept up under her shirt and vice versa, but nothing dramatic, nothing more, and yet to kiss her publicly here would imply something else, perhaps, than the simple familiarity of having kissed her before. It would be making a claim on her, of sorts. A claim she might resent. It would be telling the world that they'd spent Thursday night in a basement apartment in Queens, making out.

She reached up and kissed him softly on the mouth. Miller shivered again. "Hello," she repeated. "Are you hungry, maybe?"

Miller said that he was, and without discussion he began leading her toward a café that he knew on Gansevoort Street with sidewalk tables. He was pleased with himself for navigating the West Village with such efficiency, avoiding the wrong turns that would lead into more wrong turns and circles. Blair followed him a quarter-step behind.

They arrived to find a sidewalk table just clearing. "This looks good," Blair said. Her hair fell past her ears in a sweep of yellowish gold. She had a sweater tied around her shoulders, and under her thin white T-shirt Miller could see the outlines of her bra and her breasts. She sat down at the table and crossed her legs, strong tan legs, and motioned for Miller to sit down next to her. "Perfect," she said. "This seems perfect."

"Good," he said. "I'm glad you called." This is what satisfaction felt like. A sunny day, a beautiful girl, an available table, New York.

Naughty Bits

Blair went on to spend six nights in his apartment, but she was slow to take him home herself. She wasn't ready, she explained, to introduce him to her apartment-mates (father's housekeeper, father's cook, father himself).

"My dad gets weird around strangers," she said. It was a Friday night; they were lying in bed, and he was tracing the alphabet on her slim smooth back.

"Your dad worked in a foreign embassy," Miller said, luxuriating both in the feel of her back and in sparring with her. "He dealt with strangers for a living."

"Sure," Blair said, her voice semi-muffled by pillow. "But those are the kind of strangers my dad likes. Foreign strangers. Diplomatic strangers."

"What kind of strangers doesn't he like?"

"Strangers," Blair said, rolling over, "I might be fucking."

Miller ran a finger between her small breasts, down to her belly button. "I see."

"Mmmm," Blair said. She picked up his finger and kissed it, and then placed it back on her stomach. Miller bit his lip to keep from grinning like a fool. Three weeks and everything about Blair felt novel and delicious, like he was eating chocolate for the first time after a lifetime of bread. *Why?* Miller asked himself when she wasn't around. *What is it specifically about this girl?* He would stand in his basement and poke at the stain on the rug and bat the question around. Why her? And why not anyone else? And how does she make me so happy in the first place?

She leaned over and kissed his shoulder. "Hello," she said.

"Hello," he said.

"I'm sorry I'm so bizarre about my dad."

Miller drew a circle around her belly button. "How many of your boyfriends have met him, anyway?"

"None," Blair said. "I mean, not since high school. He can be so overbearing—I just don't know what he's going to do sometimes, whether or not he's going to behave himself. And there's never been anyone important enough to bother going through the stress of it."

"Can I meet him?" He wanted to fancy himself important.

Blair put her hand on his, stopping its descent below her navel. "Nope."

"I promise I'll be very impressive," Miller said. "Respectful. I'll call him sir."

"Who wants to be called sir?"

"Or whatever he wants to be called. Mr. Ambassador, sir. Progenitor of the wonderful Blair."

She giggled and bit his ear. "Progenitor."

"We'll talk about hobbies. The man must have hobbies. What does he like? The symphony? I know all about the goddamn symphony. We'll talk about Stravinsky."

"Joel!" She was still giggling. "Stop. I don't want to talk about my father in bed."

"Or I'll ask him about Sibelius. Stravinsky and Sibelius. He'll love me. He'll be begging you to bring me home again."

"Joel!"

"What are his hobbies?"

"He doesn't have hobbies." She pushed him off and leaned up on an elbow. "He invests in horses and art and real estate. And also baseball cards sometimes, for fun."

"Baseball cards!" Miller shouted. "Eureka!" He pushed her back down on the bed and kissed her mouth. "That's what we'll talk about. Nothing I don't know about baseball cards."

"Joel," she said. "*Basta*. Enough."

"Come on," Miller said, holding his mouth a few inches above hers. "Come on. I'll be on my best behavior." He licked her top lip, quickly.

Blair kept laughing, raised her hands lazily above her head, rested them on the pillow. Miller pinned them down with one hand and kissed her neck.

"I promise," he said. "My best behavior." He kissed her collarbone, and then her left breast, slower and slower, spending time on her small pink nipple. Blair's laughter became a short intake of breath. Miller moved on to her other breast, her other nipple, biting it gently until Blair began to whimper. He kept her hands pinned above her head.

"Man," she said softly.

He moved his head down, then, between her breasts, using his tongue to trace the pattern he'd first traced with his fingers a few minutes earlier. He kept traveling down, down, down, releasing Blair's hands and feeling them grasp at his hair, moving his head back and forth as he worked his mouth between her legs. *Good, good, good*—the word ran through his head, bouncing around his brain like a pinball. She smelled good, she tasted good, she talked good, she thought good, she looked good, she was good. She made him feel so good. "Oh, God," she whispered. "God."

Miller slid his tongue inside her, then back out. Slow, fast, slow.

"God," she whispered again. Her legs tightened and squeezed around his head; she arched her back, she called out, she came.

Soon after, she pulled him up by the elbows, and treated him to a long, sloppy kiss.

"Holy shit, Joel," she said. "Man, you're just so good."

The Keeper

Stan had over thirteen hundred baseball cards organized according to team, year, uniform number. Assuming his own passion would also be his son's, he gave Miller prized baseball cards for his fifth birthday, and presented him with finer and rarer specimens for each subsequent birthday until Miller turned fifteen and finally asked him to stop. Stan didn't understand. "Stop? But these are precious. A legacy."

"Stop. Please. Save up for a few years," Miller said. "Buy me a car when I turn seventeen. That'll be your legacy."

Stan ignored him and continued to deliver the cards, either in person, during his periodic visits, or by mail, when Miller lived in Providence and then in Queens. Once in a while a package would arrive, FedEx, and Miller would pull out a slim pack of Ozzie Smith, Jose Canseco, Bucky Dent. He put them in a shoebox under his bed and didn't think about them again until the next package came.

"So does this girl like baseball?" Stan asked Miller. They were sitting in Shea Stadium, watching the Mets lose to the Pirates. "It's important," Stan said, tearing a peanut out of its shell. "Your mother never liked baseball and that's something I didn't take enough notice of. Compatibility is important."

"Two people can be compatible without both liking baseball. Anyway, why does it matter? Blair's not mom." Bay didn't like baseball. Worse, she thought that Stan's obsession with baseball cards was better suited to a little boy than a grown man, and during those long-ago fights when she'd accuse Stan of never loving her, she threatened to seek vengeance by throwing out his cards. It was the only thing she could say to him that would make him yell.

"Look at me and your mother," Stan said. "Never might have happened had I been a little better prepared."

"Bullshit," Miller said.

"Watch your tongue."

Thirteen years after moving out of Bay's house, Stan still used his ex-wife as a reference point for everything. He grew fatter, but said it was his right, after so many years of starving ("hardly starving, dad,") on Bay's cooking. He grew grayer, but said that Bay once told him gray hair made a man look like a gentleman. He asked Miller how Bay was doing, where she was working, if she ever asked about him.

Miller told the truth, that she was fine in California, and that she never mentioned Stan's name. It was part of her homeopathic therapy in California, a program that advocated no drugs, no drinking, and no negative energy. She was not to talk about Stan anymore. Not to think about him.

Stan would rub his hands on his polo-shirted paunch and say, "Well, probably for the best, then, kid."

Donna McCrary had vanished soon after the incident in the parking lot, and since then, as far as Miller knew, his father hadn't strung together more than three dates in a row. Although Miller could well remember Donna's ridiculous Monkees tapes, and the awful candied color of her hair, he knew now that he would rather have her occupy his father than to have to watch Stan fend miserably for himself. It seemed like he was deteriorating quietly, a victim of his own benign neglect: shirts with small yellow stains, bad breath. Miller wondered if his father ever went to the doctor. He was nearing retirement. He had started sending more and more packages of baseball cards, old Topps from his collection, still in their original wrappers.

"Well, dad, I don't think Blair likes baseball that much, frankly," Miller said. "But she likes baseball cards." Stan dropped his peanuts. "She knows about baseball cards. Her father has a collection, might even be better than yours."

"Get out of here," Stan said.

"Why would I lie?"

"To try to one-up your old man," Stan said. "I know how you operate."

"No, really," Miller said. "Her father's collection is incredible, or so I hear. Makes yours look like amateur hour."

"No offense, son, but you're more full of shit than a septic tank," Stan said. "A collection better than mine. I don't believe it."

"Well, her dad has a lot of money," Miller said. "He can afford it. Honus Wagner."

"Honus Wagner? Honus *Wagner*? The most valuable card in baseball?" Stan's face flushed with awe and greed. "You're killing me, kid."

"It's true," Miller said. "Blair's offered to show me."

"Show *you*?" Stan protested. It was part of his game, the theatrical routine he had cultivated for himself in the absence of a larger vision: he was the ham, the foulmouth, the neighborhood fatso. "You're an ungrateful little schmuck!" Stan said. "What you know about cards I could fit in a pinky nail—don't look at me like that, I know you don't care. . . ."

"I don't know, dad," Miller said, jawing on a mouthful of his father's peanuts. He knew he was playing along, and assumed that his father knew it too. "Maybe if you didn't call me a schmuck I might see if Blair would show you the cards as well."

"Hmph," Stan said. A cheer went up in the crowd and then died as a foul ball flew their way. Stan raised his hand to order another beer—it was a warm evening and they were having ballpark cocktails. "Hmph," Stan said again. "Honus *Wagner*." But there was honesty in his performance. Unlike some collectors, who saw the cards as currency—were only interested in the cards they could buy and sell and own—Stan regarded baseball cards as palm-sized portals to greatness. Beholding them was enough. Miller knew what his father wanted.

"Come on," Miller said. "Maybe she'll invite us over. We can look at the cards and then go have a drink."

"Where does she live?"

"East Seventieth."

"She's fancy, this girl?"

"A little fancy," Miller said. "But you'll like her. She's smart."

"Doesn't like baseball, though."

"No," Miller said. "But she likes the cards."

Ring-a-Ding Kid

Bay called from San Francisco as the weather turned chilly. October in Queens: the leaves in Astoria Park turned maroon and orange, and stores put pumpkins in their windows. The Mets had come close, but blew it against the Braves in the second round of the play-offs. Stan and Miller sat in the stands and got rained on for fifteen innings. Blair bought Miller a turtleneck sweater. Grant bought the loft in Tribeca and began planning his housewarming party.

"So you haven't been calling," Bay accused.

"I've been busy," Miller said.

"Too busy to call?"

"There's a lot going on," Miller said.

"You're happy?"

"I'm happy."

"Then call me once in a while to let me know that you're happy," Bay said. "Your father called."

"What?" Miller lit a cigarette. Blair was curled up and sleeping on his ratty orange sofa. "What do you mean, my father called? I thought you guys weren't supposed to be in phone contact."

"Hey, you're telling me. I haven't said a word to that man since the day you graduated from college." Miller well remembered that little nightmare, his parents sitting next to each other during the ceremony, holding forced conversations with the people sitting on either side, trying to reinforce the public notion that they were strangers.

"What did he want?"

"Just to talk," Bay said. "He just wanted to talk to me. He didn't say anything in particular."

"Is he all right?"

"I was going to ask you that."

"He's seemed okay to me lately. I mean, the usual bullshit, but okay."

"Watching his weight?"

"Not really."

"He should be. That's what I said to him: I said, Stanley, you have a son who will make us grandparents one day. I want you to be around to see your grandkids."

"What did he say?"

"He thanked me," Bay said, "for worrying. Honestly, honey, it sounded like he just needed someone to talk to."

After he hung up, Miller woke Blair by tickling her feet. "Can my dad see your father's baseball cards?" It had been over a month since he'd made that promise to Stanley, a promise that he'd quickly forgotten.

Blair rubbed an eye and looked at him quizzically. "Can your dad what?"

"He's all by himself in New Jersey," Miller said. "He loves baseball cards. I told him once about your father's and he got all lit up. I don't know. Plus, he's heard a lot about you. He wants to meet you."

"You told your dad a lot about me?" Blair smiled and took a drag of Miller's cigarette. She was picking up a few bad habits from him. "Well then," she said. "I'll see what I can do."

Three days later, Blair called Miller at the office. He loved it when she did this; it seemed to him like a public confirmation of their relationship. Sometimes it was all he could do not to press SPEAKERPHONE and let everyone else in the BigFunCity warren of cubicles hear the lilting voice of his girl. "What's up?" he asked her.

"Well, Reynold's going to be out of town next week, some

kind of function in Salzburg," she said. "But maybe it'll be better that way."

"Better for what?" Miller asked. He rested the receiver between his head and shoulder and leaned back with his feet on the desk. Company rumor had it that he was soon to be promoted to literary editor, and lately Miller had been practicing the part.

"You know, for someone who claims to care about his father, you have a really shitty memory about the things you've promised him. Baseball cards, remember? Your father can come to the apartment if he wants. I cleared it with my dad. This Friday."

"Shit, of course," Miller said. He raised his voice a little so that Jed Hilary, the jackal who sat in the cubicle to the right, would be able to hear. "Baby, that's so great of you to remember my pops."

"Who are you talking to?" Blair said.

"I'm talking to you," Miller said.

Blair laughed. "I'm not your baby," she said. "And your father is definitely not your pops, Mr. Ring-a-Ding-Ding. Tell him we're on for Friday at seven thirty, and also tell him to bring some gloves. We're not allowed to touch the cards without gloves."

"Sure," Miller said, as Blair's extension clicked off. "Baby." He raised his voice slightly now that she was gone, imagining himself in a rumpled tuxedo with his arm around Blair and a cigarette burning in his hand.

"Who you talking to there, Mills?" asked Jed Hilary from behind his plasterboard partition.

"Talking to my girl, Jed," said Miller. "I'm just talking to my girl." He placed the phone back on the receiver, snapped his fingers crisply, and then pointed to the air in front of him. He winked. Ring-a-ding kid, he thought to himself. Baby, here's to you.

Paterfamilias

"Gloves," Stan said. "That's ridiculous."

"Those are the rules." Miller was at the Fort Lee condo on Thursday night, having agreed to Stan's spontaneous invitation. They were eating Chinese and watching TV. Though the weather was brisk and the apartment cool, Stan was sweating through his T-shirt and gulping water furiously.

"Kung Pao chicken," Stan said. "Goddamn, that's spicy."

Miller jabbed at a chunk of chicken with his chopsticks. "Not really, dad."

"Not really?" Stan said. "Your chest get hairier or something, kid? This is spicy stuff." He lifted the carton of rice to his mouth and poured it in as though it were liquid. After all these years, Miller was still amazed at his father's oblivious capacity. "Spicy stuff."

"You should slow down when you eat, dad. You'll get heartburn."

"What are you, my mother?" Stan said. He wiped his hands on his pants. "So tell me about Blair's cards."

"Well, like I said, it's one hell of a collection. Her father invests in this stuff, you understand. It's not just for recreation."

"So really big-time, huh?"

"Yessir," Miller said. "Big-time."

Stan raised an eyebrow. "She involved in any monkey business?"

"What are you talking about?"

His eyebrow still raised, Stan gave an exaggerated shrug, as if to suggest that the world of baseball cards was dark and full of danger.

"Give me a break, dad."

"Look, I've just never heard of having to wear gloves to a private residence, is all. I'm just thinking it sounds a little crazy."

"Blair's dad is eccentric."

Stan sighed, and with some audible effort pushed himself off the couch and headed to the kitchenette for a beer.

Miller sank back into the chubby leather of his father's couch, enjoying the slightly illicit sensation of drowning in all that animal skin. He took in the unapologetic bachelor-ness of his father's apartment, a fact that on some level never surprised him, and yet on another delivered a small jolt every time he visited. The place smelled like coffee and air freshener. The carpet was thin gray, the apartment complex's cheapest carpeting option. And more, too: the black leather couch, leather ottoman, leather armchair, the high-definition television, the dead potted plant in the corner. Nothing on the walls save a framed photograph of Stan's mother, who died of breast cancer when Stan was a teenager. In the picture, Stan's mother is leaning over her son—then a fat, smiling baby—and wiping food off his chin. She is wearing a dainty scarf around her neck and a wide flared skirt.

"You think about your mom much, dad?" Miller asked, standing to take a closer look at the picture. The way she was posed, he could see only her profile, but there was something of Stan hidden in there, the same full cheeks and small ears. Miller wondered why he'd never asked before, and also how it was that he knew nothing of his grandmother besides the fact that once upon a time she wore scarves and skirts to feed her only child.

Stan returned from the kitchenette with a frosted Coors in each hand, settled back down on the couch and handed Miller a beer. "What do you want to know about my mother?"

"Why don't you ever talk about her? I mean, her picture's right here."

"Well, of course I keep her picture," Stan said. Miller sat down on the floor, cross-legged. "She was my mother."

"But you don't talk about her much."

"You don't talk about your own mother much," Stan said.

"You know that's different."

"Huh," Stan said. He looked over Miller's head at the television. The Knicks were losing, so he switched it off with a flick of the remote. He smiled ruefully at his son. "I don't talk about her much, that's true. But my mother was an unhappy woman. From what I remember, anyway. Even when she was healthy she didn't smile much."

"How come?"

"I don't know." Stan sighed. "What's with this curiosity?"

Miller looked over at the picture again. There was silence but for Stan's noises—he could never be wholly quiet, and so there was always some breathing or snorting or sniffling to contend with or ignore. Now Stan cleared his throat and said, "I'll tell you about my mother. If you're asking."

Miller nodded, lifted his beer.

"Well, in most of my memories, she's in the kitchen. She used to start making breakfast for my father at six in the morning, had his dinner ready at six o'clock every night. You could set a clock by it. Packed brown bag lunches for my dad to take to work. In the afternoons, she smoked cigarettes in the kitchen, did the crossword."

"Did you feel close to her?"

"Close?" Stan scratched his cheek. "It was tough—she wasn't the sort of woman you could feel close to. She never said anything, really. Followed my father around with a pot roast in her hands, let him do all the talking. She was sort of like a mystery I wasn't interested in." Stan scratched his cheek again. "I have my regrets, of course. But I was a teenager when she got sick. And teenagers are stupid, son, and that's a fact. I didn't know any better."

"You were a teenager when she died?"

"Fifteen. She died in just a year. Got sick, got the diagnosis, and then just lay in bed till death took her away like a blind date." Stan sighed. "My dad, well, you probably don't remember him, but I'll tell you—he was in a panic. Had no idea what he'd do without her. She was his maid and his cook and his only friend."

What could Miller remember of his grandfather? A drawn man in a brown suit, a silver crew cut. The scratchy feel of stubble when he was pulled in for a hug. Miller's grandfather lived in a dark apartment in Newark, and spent his last years railing against the neighborhood's newcomers, with their dirty children and their Spanish smells and their incomprehensible music. When Miller visited him, the old man would take him to the decrepit candy store on the corner and buy him Tootsie Rolls by the bagful. He died when Miller was eight.

"So after my mother got sick, my father brought home the craziest what-have-you. Herb teas and chicken feet and crap from Chinatown. Whatever he heard might do the trick. I remember my mother just staring at him, not drinking the tea, not lighting the candles. My father was not a superstitious man, but he was willing to try anything. Desperation. They called her illness calcification of the breast. And my father would have done anything to make her get well. But my mother refused to even try."

Miller had heard the skeleton of this story over the years without ever thinking to ask for further details, but sitting on his father's floor he felt a thrill of interest in his own history. There were questions he wanted answered, although he was not sure that Stanley would know what to say: Why did his grandmother give up so easily? Didn't she want to watch her son become an adult? Did she love her husband at all?

His curiosity was shaping itself into an idea: that he was linked, across generations, to thousands of unhappy women. "You still angry about her?" he asked.

Stan took a sip of beer. "Tell you the truth, I'm sixty-one years old and I think about my mother all the time. My father never got over it. Before he lost my mother he weighed a deuce and a half," he said. "After she died, he became like a skeleton."

After a long silence, Miller said, "Blair's mother died too. When she was a child. Blair barely remembers her."

Stan gave Miller a funny look. "Lovely," he said. He turned the television back on. "Then she and I'll have something to talk about."

• • •

That night, in his Queens basement, Miller called Bay. It was one in the morning, but the time difference worked to his advantage. Bay picked up the phone on the third ring.

"I had dinner with dad tonight," he said.

"This is what you're calling to tell me in the middle of the night?"

"Did he ever talk to you about his mother?"

"You woke me up," Bay said.

Miller lit a Camel Light and sat down on the stain on his rug. "Just . . . come on, mom. I'm curious. We talked about her tonight and I realized I had never heard anything about her and I was curious."

"You should stop smoking," Bay said.

Miller inhaled. "I know."

There was a pause.

"He still has that picture of her?"

"Yeah. I noticed it tonight like I had never seen it before."

Bay chuckled. "Here's what you would know about your father if you were a little more observant. He's a devoted man. He loves his women. But he's not great at real life, at dealing with real problems. You've seen it."

"That's what happened to you guys," Miller said. "He couldn't handle your problems."

"A lot happened with us guys," Bay said. "It wasn't just that I misbehaved. Don't you try to blame it on me."

"I know, mom," he said. "I wasn't blaming you." He was trying to imagine his mother in her San Francisco apartment, a place that he had never seen, a city he had never visited. He knew what San Francisco looked like, though, from movies and friends' descriptions, and in his head he saw his mother in a Victorian house on top of a steep hill where all the cars were parked at an angle.

"What do you know?" Bay said. "You never ask any questions, you never pay enough attention. You know nothing at all. Your father put me through hell for years. I never would have broken down if he hadn't—"

"Mom," Miller said. He wasn't in the mood for her revisionism. "Not now."

"Well, excuse me, Mr. Sensitive," Bay said. "If you didn't want to hear, you shouldn't have asked." And with a muttered good-bye, she hung up.

In the Cards

The next night, Friday, seven o'clock, Miller picked up his father at the George Washington Bridge bus terminal and together they hailed a cab for East Seventieth Street. Stan looked entirely different than he had the night before, dressed in a double-breasted gray suit and inky shined shoes. The suit seemed brand-new, just a bit too tight, and Miller worried that his father had actually driven to the mall and shopped today. Stan had gone overboard. A pair of thin black gloves poked out of his breast pocket, and he was carrying a bouquet of yellow roses. "For your girl," he said.

"Is that a new suit?"

"I needed one," Stan said. Miller did not believe him.

"You could have found one in the right size, at least."

Stan looked at Miller curiously. He adjusted his dark striped tie. "This is my size."

Miller had never been to Blair's apartment before, and he was nervous. He himself had changed clothing several times (and knew he shouldn't judge Stan so severely), for he'd imagined that hidden cameras would record his image and upload them to a judgmental and severe Reynold Carter. Or, perhaps, that one of the Park Avenue servants doubled as a spy. Paradoxically, Miller felt with an uncomfortable surety that Blair's father had never even heard of him, and if he had, could care less. He'd decided on khakis and a thin brown sweater.

Reynold Carter's house in the Hamptons had been large and airy, but also casual, the architectural equivalent of designer jeans. Miller was expecting the Park Avenue place to be a tuxedo, with columns and marble and a baby grand piano. Miller had formed his idea of what the finer things looked like as a child by listening to Bay coo over the fancier houses in their neighborhood, the ones with Ionic detailing and pilasters.

"You look like you swallowed a lemon, kid," Stan said. He was sitting back like a pasha on the cab's torn vinyl seat.

Miller fiddled with the pack of Camel Lights in his jacket pocket. "Are you gonna pick on me all night, dad?"

"Are you gonna pick on me?" Stan said. "Sit straight."

Stan gazed out the window at the trees of Central Park, dignified, content. Despite the tightness of the suit and the too-wide cut of the tie, he managed to seem powerful in the back of the cab. It crossed Miller's mind that his father ought to have been a more successful man. As it was, in the back of a cab, holding a bouquet for a beautiful woman, he played the part of success surprisingly well.

• • •

The building was prim and gray and serious, like an expression of displeasure. The liveried doorman opened the door for Stan and Miller with swift efficiency. "Carter, please," Miller said as they stepped into a bright white lobby filled with flowers. The elevator, a crenellated mahogany box, took them up sixteen flights to the penthouse.

"Right on time!" Blair said when she opened the door. Her presence was somehow disorienting to Miller, that this woman who appeared so often in Queens in sneakers and torn T-shirts should now be standing at the massive door, smiling pleasantly, wearing a slim gray dress and pearls. "Blair Carter," she said, extending her hand to Stan.

"Stanley Miller," he said, looking, to Miller's astonishment, utterly relaxed. "These are for you." He handed her the roses.

"Oh, how beautiful," she said, putting them to her nose. "Thank you. Please come in."

Miller felt like he had just walked into a Noël Coward play, Stan and Blair both in roles he had never previously seen them perform. The apartment itself was different than he had expected, almost as airy as the Bridgehampton place, with enormous abstract paintings on the walls and asymmetrical metal sculptures planted on the floor like random tombstones. Miller looked around for some intimation of what Blair's life here was like. A photograph, a memento on a side table, even a smell to suggest cooking or bathing or cleaning up. But everything in the apartment was austere and unrevealing.

"And what's this?" Stan asked in an admiring tone, heading toward a white canvas with a black square on it.

"It's a wonderful picture," Blair said. "Ellsworth Kelly. My father got it at auction before Kelly's stuff went through the roof." They all stared intently at the painting—the "picture"—Blair smiling, Stan affecting a connoisseur's regard, and Miller wondering if his father really did appreciate this plain black square on this plain white background. He would have suspected that this painting was just the sort of thing Stan would insist any three-year-old had the talent to produce.

"Shall we go look at the cards, gentlemen?" Blair asked, after a few more respectful moments in front of the Kelly. "Did everyone bring their gloves?" Stan plucked the pair from his pocket and flexed his fingers before putting them on. Blair pulled on a pair of white cotton gloves and turned to Miller. "What about you?"

Miller reddened. "I wasn't planning on touching them," he said.

"You forgot?" Blair asked.

"How could you forget, son?"

Oh, get off my goddamn case, Miller thought. "I don't know, pops, I just figured I'd leave the handling to you."

Beyond the front room was another room, similarly anonymous, with more large paintings and spiky sculptures. Blair sat down on one of the low backless couches in the center and made a sweeping gesture with her hand. Stan sat down in an armless armchair and, with a slight toss of his head, loosened his necktie. Miller had no idea where to sit. Blair, already making small talk with Stan, did not indicate that Miller should sit next to her. But if he took the couch opposite, he might seem distant or strange. He began to sweat.

"Sit down, won't you, son?"

"Right." Miller sat down on the same stiff horsehair couch as Blair, but kept his butt a good foot or so from hers. He felt contained in his own small box of discomfort: he did not even know the right way to sit. And here he was, with his girl!

Blair's legs were crossed at the ankles, and she was turned delicately toward Stan, leaning in just barely. Stan was beaming. Miller wondered how long it had been since his father had been on the receiving end of such adoring female attention.

There was a large black leather-lined binder on the table in front of them. "I had this taken out this morning," Blair said, stroking the top of the binder with a slim finger in the white glove. Miller scooted in closer to her by a fraction. He felt himself suddenly aroused. "My father keeps this case in a safe. This is the best of the bunch."

"Terrific," Stan said, rubbing his hands together as if in anticipation of a fine meal. "I'll tell you, Blair, this is a treat for me. A real treat."

"I'm so glad," Blair said, removing her finger from the top of the binder and placing it, for a whisper of a second, on Stan's gray lapel. It was a gesture that could have been missed in a blink, but neither Stan nor Miller was blinking.

Reynold Carter's Top Four Specimens of Baseball History, Lovingly Presented by His Daughter and Admired by Stanley B. Miller:

1. A 1911 Tyrus Raymond Cobb, Cobb wearing a pristine Detroit Tigers uniform, set against a field of green and orange. He was depicted mid-swing, his cap small and almost yarmulke-like, his face bony and angular. "The cards were advertisements, you know," Blair said. "For cigarettes. And also for a while they served to help stiffen the cigarette pack, back when cigarettes were mostly sold in soft packs." Miller reached into his pocket for a Camel Light and then remembered where he was. Stan nodded proudly at Blair, like a parent.
2. An 1887 full color of Hardie Henderson, pitcher for the Brooklyn Trolley Dodgers, notable as much for its relative age and full-color majesty as for the fame of the player depicted. On the card, only a mere 2.8 x 1.5 inches, floated a portrait of the mustachioed Henderson, looking like nothing so much as the third man in a barbershop quartet. Underneath the portrait, in miniature, was an image of Henderson winding a pitch as batter and catcher waited in the distance. "A beaut," Stan said in appreciative tones.
3. A real, honest-to-God, 1910 Honus Wagner, an original T-206 from the American Tobacco Company, although not, Blair admitted with a sad shrug, the "Great One." The "Great One" was the only T-206 in dealer-approved mint condition, which had previously been in the hands of hockey legend Wayne Gretzky

and was now owned by a fanatic collector from the Midwest who had recently put it on the market for a reputed $2.5 million. "Too rich for our blood," Blair said, although Miller wondered if that could possibly be true.

4. And finally, the triple. Entombed in plastic, staring ahead somberly as if hearing extremely bad news, were the three broad-foreheaded visages of the best double-play combination in baseball history: Joe Tinker, Johnny Evers, and Frank Chance. The trio plied their trade with the Chicago Cubs at the beginning of the century, leading Chicago to four National League pennants (1906, 1907, 1908, and 1910) and two World Series wins (in 1907 and 1908). The Baseball Hall of Fame inducted the three simultaneously in 1946. When confronted with this perfectly preserved triad of myth, Stan let out a hearty sigh. "This," he said, "is a small miracle." Then, without preamble, he closed his eyes and recited:

> *"These are the saddest of possible words:*
> *'Tinker to Evers to Chance.'*
> *Trio of bear cubs, and fleeter than birds,*
> *Tinker and Evers and Chance.*
> *Ruthlessly pricking our gonfalon bubble,*
> *Making a Giant hit into a double—*
> *Words that are heavy with nothing but trouble:*
> *'Tinker to Evers to Chance.' "*

"Dad?" Miller said. His father, shining his shoes, appreciating modern art, reciting poetry! So this was how Stan had spent all these years schmoozing doctors and pharmaceutical executives. Miller could not have been more impressed. "Dad?"

Stanley opened his eyes. "The world," he said. "Let me tell

you something, kid. The world . . ." Stan looked off into the distance, as though he had just seen something beautiful there.

"Yeah?" Miller asked.

"The world," Stan said, "it used to be a better place."

• • •

They repaired to a bar off Madison Avenue, filled with votive candles and tall red flowers and unsmiling women. Blair got them a table in a quiet spot near the window and ordered a round of martinis.

"Ah," Stan said. "I haven't had a good martini in ages." Miller thought to himself that Blair could have suggested a piss on the rocks and Stan would have given her the thumbs-up. He put his hand on Blair's leg, but it felt wrong and he took it away.

"So tell me about the cards, Blair," Stan said as their martinis were delivered. "How'd your father dig those up, anyway?"

Blair shrugged. "You know, I really have no idea."

"You don't know?" Stan lifted his martini and took a healthy sip. "I've gotta tell you, it's not so easy to find cards like that. You really should ask your dad how he did it."

"We don't talk much about things like that," Blair said. "We don't really talk about process."

"Process?" Stan chortled. With every sip of the booze, he was becoming more and more like his old self. "Who the hell talks about process? What's a process?"

"You know, how things get done. My father is very secretive."

"Secretive," Stan said, and put his fist over his mouth as if to suppress a burp. "I must tell you, kids, that it's not a bad thing for a man to be secretive. Keeps him out of trouble."

"Then you must not know how to keep secrets, dad," Miller said.

"Never kept one in my life." Stan chuckled. He plucked an

olive out of his martini and plopped it in his mouth like so much fish food.

"Then answer me this," Miller said. "Did you really like that painting of a square? I mean, no offense, Blair, but . . ."

"I'm a sophisticated man," Stan said.

"Stop the bullshit."

"Hell," Stanley muttered, and cuffed his son lightly on the arm. "I took an art history course," he said. "For your mother. Years and years ago, before I married her. She wanted me to have a little class, you know, couldn't just stay some schlump from Weequahic." He picked up his martini and chuckled to himself. "She wanted me to know about *painters*," he said. "I had to take her to the *opera*."

"You took mom to the opera?"

"Well, not exactly. The opera was pretty expensive, and we were saving our money for the house in Heyward. But I bought her some records she said she wanted. Verdi, you know. *Rigoletto*."

Blair was nodding and grinning at Stan, a bit too flirtatiously for Miller's taste.

"I never in my life heard either one of you listen to Verdi," he said.

"Neither of us could really stand the stuff," Stan said. "But you know your mother. She wanted us to have a little sophistication." Stan sipped the last of his martini a bit mournfully. "Without her I'd probably be just another asshole selling drug samples from the trunk of a Ford."

"You're no asshole, Stan," Blair said, and Stanley beamed. "I wish I could talk to my own father the way that you two talk."

"You can't talk to your father?" Miller said. "I always had the idea that you guys were so close."

"Well, you know." Blair gave another flirty shrug. "He's a busy man."

"Lucky for him," Stan said. "It's good to be busy. Staying busy keeps you fit, keeps you young." Stan pinched Blair lightly on her upper arm. She giggled.

As the next round of martinis was finished and the hours ticked by, they switched to a different bar, down the block, an Irish place where Stan ordered them all burgers and beer. He was expansive, drunk; charming Blair with stories of fishing for sea bass with cardiologists in California and playing golf with nephrologists in Texas. He told her about growing up in the Weequahic section of Newark when that city still had large pockets of the middle class, and about how he skipped out of fourth-grade classes to watch the Dodgers-Yankees World Series in 1947.

"Skipped class? Didn't you get in trouble?"

"Nah." Stan laughed, waving away Miller's cigarette smoke. "When my dad found out, he was about as proud of me as he'd ever been. Said at least I had my priorities straight."

Blair took a drag of Miller's cigarette. She was beaming proudly, as though Stan's stories were about her own family, as though Stan's hijinks were her own.

• • •

On the phone that night, Bay was unsurprised. "Well, of course," she said to Miller. He could hear her snap her gum from three thousand miles away. She was trying to quit smoking. "You must know your father always did have a thing for young girls."

What Separates Us from the Beasts

Three nights later, on the futon, Blair said, "I liked Stanley."

"He liked you too." Miller had just eased himself into her, too soon really, as she was dry and tight. But she had been lying there groggy and half-naked and Miller couldn't help himself. It was late at night and the Knicks had won at home. They had drank three Negra Modelos apiece and listened to the game on the radio. After, once they had brushed their teeth, Miller leaned over and parted her knees with his hands. He kissed the space between her eyes.

"He's lonely, though."

"Let's not talk about my dad right now," Miller said. He kissed her neck, moved slowly in and out. She was quiet for a minute. Miller picked up the pace, trying to find the right balance between feeling pleasure and coming too fast.

"It's a weird thing, isn't it?"

"What is?" he asked.

"This. You. Inside me."

"What do you mean?"

Blair sighed, a distinctly unaroused sigh. Miller felt himself wilt a little. Blair was on the pill and they had stopped using condoms after their joint AIDS tests a few weeks ago. Fucking her bareback still felt like a rare privilege. "It's just strange," she said, "to contain another body inside mine."

"It's just my dick," Miller said.

"I know," Blair said. She moved her hips a little, which Miller took as a cue to move his own. Soon they were achieving a nice rhythm, and he hoped she wouldn't keep talking. But then:

"It's just so animal, isn't it? All this rutting."

"Do you want me to stop?" Miller asked.

"No," she said. "It's okay. I just think it's important to consider the act."

"I consider the act all the time," Miller said, planting his mouth on hers. He decided it would probably be best to come before she completely ruined the mood.

"There's actually very little that separates us from the beasts."

Miller swallowed any response. He moved his hips faster and faster, feeling his balls tighten, his heart speed up.

"I mean, this is what we do, feed ourselves, fuck, sleep. Piss and shit. What's the difference between us, really, and, say, dogs?"

Miller felt his palms sweat and his dick expand inside her slick warmth.

"We're animals, honestly. It's so outrageous. This proves it."

"What?"

"We're beasts." There was something in her tone, a mixture of cynicism and perplexity, that sent Miller over the edge. He came in great sweeping spasms, crying out into her shoulder. A minute or two later, he rolled over and stared up at the basement ceiling.

"I think that you should get a pet."

If she was being hostile, Miller preferred not to notice. He waited for his breathing to regulate. "Sounds good to me."

Dog Days

And so Miller liberated Harry from the medieval cages of the Ninety-sixth Street ASPCA, and the dog's impact was immediate. It felt like a renewal. Blair and Miller were thrilled. They talked about the dog incessantly, what he ate, how often he shat, whether or not he was putting on weight. Blair had never before owned a pet, and Miller wondered what had taken her so long to have a dog in her life. She came over at odd times to walk Harry, and took charge of his grooming and his veterinary needs.

They stopped having their most important conversations in bed, and began talking about the important things on walks with Harry around Queens, strolling at a leisurely pace, allowing the dog to luxuriate in smells he had been denied and sights he had missed during those monastic months in the ASPCA. While they walked, Blair told Miller about the architecture of the many churches they were passing, the Romanesque and the Moderne. She bought them baklava at a Turkish bakery and reminisced about the summer she and her father toured Turkey with members of the diplomatic corps. She daydreamed out loud about traveling to new places. She asked Miller questions about what Harry did when she wasn't around, but she also asked him about other things: to whom he had lost his virginity, what were the best things he could imagine eating on a piece of pizza, why he preferred short women to tall ones, what kind of kid he had been.

"What kind of kid?"

"Yeah," she said. They had made it all the way to the water, and the grassy slope of Astoria Park.

"I don't know," Miller said, genuinely stumped. "I was just like any other kid, I guess. Kind of dorky. I always had my head in some book or another."

"You still have your head in some book or another."

"Reading's a hard habit to break," Miller said. He was currently on a Martin Amis tear, finishing up *Money*, which Grant had correctly promised that he'd love. "And, as you know, I still haven't gotten around to buying a television."

"You're a weird duck, Miller," Blair said.

"Really?" He kissed her on the cheek. "I always thought I was pretty conventional. No weird tics or diseases, normal height, normal weight, just a little myopic. . . ."

"Actually, you're a bit skinny."

"I don't want to take over the world; I don't even want a big piece of the world. Just want to do my job and get my paycheck and take care of my girl."

"Noble aspirations."

"I always thought so," Miller said.

They both watched as Harry strained at his leash to chase a pigeon.

"Well, I was a serious kid," Blair offered, after a moment. "Very serious. I never smiled. I never felt comfortable. Even around my father or the nanny, I could never totally relax. I needed everything to be perfect and I felt like if anything at all got fucked up, it was somehow my fault."

"You were a perfectionist," Miller said.

"No," Blair countered. "I was a neurotic. I always felt like I had to take charge, make sure everybody was happy. And if somebody was unhappy, I took it personally."

"Were *you* happy?" Miller asked.

"Rarely."

"Are you happy now?" He asked her this question with a sort of egotistical confidence, assuming that because the time he spent with her was, in most ways, the happiest time he had ever known, the glow of happiness that surrounded him would also by necessity surround her. He expected reciprocation.

It was quite a surprise when Blair answered. "Happy?" she said quietly. "I really don't know."

Companionship

And it was even more of a surprise when Stan announced that he was going back to Blair's house for further inspection of Reynold Carter's card collection. "She called me last night," he said, peeling the label off a chilly Budweiser with a sheepish expression on his face. "Said she wanted to go through more of her father's cards with me. Wanted me to give her more information. What was I gonna say, no?"

They were sitting at Floyd's Midnight Cantina just off Route 4 in Fort Lee. It was dark inside the bar, but outside it was a very pleasant twilight, six in the evening, a warm Sunday in October. They had been drinking Buds for two hours now and eating stale popcorn from dented metal bowls on the bar. On the twin televisions overhead MTV played soundlessly. The jukebox played the Doors.

Miller jiggled some popcorn in his hand. "So you're just going to go up to her apartment and look through her father's stuff?"

"Well, from the sound of it, her father's going to be away," Stan said.

"So it'll be just the two of you," Miller said.

"Jealous, son?"

"Please," Miller said, and tried to approximate a chortle, but the sound caught in his throat and he had to wash it down with Bud.

"Listen, there's nothing to be worried about," Stan said. "I'm not there to, you know, horn in on your territory. Now, of course I will admit that your Blair is a very lovely woman, I mean a real pretty girl, but there's no misintentions on my part, I can promise you. I have no interest in horning in."

"That's very nice, dad."

"Really, son," Stan said. "That's the truth." Stan was still picking at the Budweiser label, but he was grinning, and Miller knew that he was secretly relishing this, the prospect of a few hours in a fancy apartment with his son's girlfriend, a twenty-six-year-old blonde.

"You're no threat, if that's what you're thinking," Miller said. "Believe me."

"Okay, son."

"She just wants to know about the cards. She wants to impress her father—impressing her father is very important to her."

"So she's going to use your father to impress her own father?" Stan said.

"Something like that," Miller said, and turned his attention to MTV. What the hell was this, anyway? Why hadn't Blair mentioned it? His father and his girlfriend in cahoots? And since when was Stan such an expert, anyway, that he could be the scholar-in-residence at Blair's house? It was bullshit. "So when are you planning this little excursion?"

"Maybe at the end of the week," Stan said, and then caught Miller's eye. He picked a blackened kernel of popcorn from the bowl and cracked it between his teeth. "Don't mope, kid. I'm just gonna tell her a little about baseball. Give her a couple life lessons."

"Life lessons? Since when are you equipped to give anyone a lesson on anything, much less life?"

Stan didn't respond, and just as quickly as Miller had felt angry he now felt ashamed. Stan refused to meet his eyes. "I'm your father," he said after a moment. "You should behave with a little more respect."

Exercising Demons

Grant liked to jog down in Battery Park most mornings at six o'clock sharp. Miller had yet to accept his friend's invitation to run alongside, as a pack-and-a-half-a-day habit did little to improve his physical stamina, and anyway Miller was left cold by the thought of rising from his bed to meet Grant before dawn. But after returning from drinking in New Jersey with Stan, Miller couldn't sleep. At two in the morning he turned on Yo La Tengo and lay on his futon with his eyes closed, imagining Blair and Stan together. She was wearing her baseball cap and a T-shirt with the neck cut off; he was in a brand-new suit. They were drinking martinis, they were drinking Coronas, she was making him a salad. What did she want from him? The clock clicked past two, two thirty, three in the morning. They were laughing together over something funny Stanley said. Why did she think Stan was so charming? Harry climbed up on the futon and put his heavy head on Miller's stomach.

At ten after five, still wide awake, Miller laced up his green Converse low-tops and headed for Battery Park. At this hour Astoria was dark, quiet, and cold. Miller fought the urge to light a cigarette. He zipped up his jacket and descended into the Steinway Street station, alongside a Mexican lady with a baby on her hip.

Forty minutes later he found Grant doing warm-ups at the northern end of the Battery Park esplanade. "Good morning." Grant was bending over to touch his toes, his legs wrapped in black spandex, like an off-hour ballerina.

"What the fuck are you doing here, sunshine?"

"Couldn't sleep."

"Insomnia?" Grant said. "What's the problem? Are you sick?"

"No."

"Still getting laid?"

"Yes," Miller said, although actually it had been a week since he had seen Blair, and in the past few days he'd been jerking off more than usual, but guiltily, when Harry wasn't looking.

"What are you eating?" Grant said, lunging forward, balancing his right foot on a bench. "You've got to cut out the wheat, I'm telling you. Lean proteins: you want chicken breasts, salmon fillets. No more spaghetti and meatballs. And watch the alcohol intake."

"I'm eating okay."

Grant switched feet, lunged forward again. "Depressed? You get depressed, your world falls apart, you can't eat, can't fuck, can't sleep. Nothing."

"I know, Grant. I'm not depressed."

"So what's the problem?" Grant jumped up and down twice, little hops, and then began to jog in place. Miller jogged along, his toes pushing against the front of his sneakers.

"I think my father wants to have an affair with Blair."

Grant chuckled. "You're crazy. Let's go." He turned and began running down the esplanade. There were others jogging easily in front of them. Miller felt like a chump; he was already wheezing and his Salvation Army shorts were giving him a wedgie.

"Blair made a date to see my dad. Says she wants to talk about baseball cards, which is bullshit, since I know she couldn't care less about baseball cards."

"So what do you think she wants?"

"I have no idea," Miller said. "I mean, I can't imagine she would actually want to have sex with my father. The man is no Cary Grant."

"Actually, I remember Stan was a captivating guy."

"Gimme a break." Miller was gasping. "Let's stop for a second." He knelt to catch his breath.

"I'm just saying, you should hand it to him a little. I remember his bachelor pad out in Fort Lee. He had his shit hooked up." Grant jogged in place at Miller's side. His T-shirt clung to his biceps.

"And therefore Blair might find my overweight, sixty-something fuck of a father sexually appealing?"

"I'm just saying anything's possible" Grant said. His eyes followed the ass of a tall blonde in gray leggings.

"Do you mind if we walk a little?"

"Don't be a pussy." Grant broke once more into a jog. "And don't freak out. Blair is not going to fuck your father. It's not happening."

"Look, it's just that she didn't say anything to me. She doesn't even know I know he's going out there."

"So what?"

"So it's weird that she's keeping a secret. It makes the whole thing mysterious."

"It's no big deal. Maybe she wants to impress her father with some baseball-card knowledge she can sponge off your dad. Or maybe she wants to get to know Stan so she can become part of your family. Or maybe she just has a thing for old men. Who knows?"

"A thing for old men?" Miller said miserably.

"You've got to ask her. You'll never know what's going on until you ask her." To the east, over downtown Brooklyn, the sun was beginning to rise.

"Perhaps you speak the truth, Grant."

"Of course I do." The Hudson was sparkling with early morning light, and ferries were already beginning to cross in from New Jersey.

"My father seems to really like her, though. You should see him around her; he's almost giddy."

"Well, sure. Just because he's your father doesn't make him blind. Blair's a strange bird, but she's cute."

"I think I'm falling in love with her," Miller said, and then wished he hadn't. He was panting and delirious with exhaustion, however, and his defenses were down.

"Love?" Grant said. "With Blair? A girl you don't even know how to talk to?" He shook his head. "You should be more careful." Then Grant broke into a run that left Miller with his hands on his knees, wheezing. He gasped twice, coughed up something off-white and sticky, and then hobbled along the esplanade after his friend.

Curry

Two nights later, Blair showed up around dinnertime, holding a bag of vegetables. A surprise. "Let's cook dinner," she said. "I feel like curry." She was wearing a tight denim skirt that reminded Miller of high school girls and blow jobs in station wagons. Adjusting his jeans and straightening his glasses, Miller walked to Ahmed's Sundries on Thirty-first Street. He returned with a can of coconut milk, a tube of curry paste, two stalks of lemongrass, and a bag of mushrooms. There were peppers and eggplant and a small, shiny zucchini, which Blair prepared in her inimitable way.

He put his hand on her shoulder as she sliced vegetables into inch-long strips; he inhaled the pungent garlic and ginger simmering on his stove. There was rice steaming in the steamer she had given him for occasions such as this, and two open beers on the remaining space of the kitchen counter.

Miller kissed the top of Blair's head and closed his eyes.

"Stop," Blair said. "I need to concentrate."

Miller grabbed his beer and went over to the CD player. He put on Stevie Wonder, *Songs in the Key of Life*, and hummed along to "Isn't She Lovely." Tendrils of steam began issuing from the kitchen area, carrying with them the funky, sexy smell of curry. Harry woke from a nap and Blair fed him three biscuits and a dropped piece of pepper. He licked her calf in gratitude.

They arranged themselves on the floor, with forks and spoons and napkins spread out on the carpet, Harry between them, shaggy head propped on his paws, whining for food. They ate quickly, and shared a cigarette after.

"Did you have a nice time with my dad?" Miller asked, getting up to clear the dirty plates. The food and music had warmed him, and he tried to ask the question kindly.

"Your dad?"

"He mentioned that he was going to stop by your apartment," Miller said. "Something about baseball cards." He watched her face to see if he was hitting any particular nerve.

"Sure." Blair pressed her thumb down on a grain of rice. "On Sunday. Your dad said he had some business in the city anyway, so he came by and we looked at the rest of my father's cards."

"And how was it?"

"Sweet," Blair said. "He told me more about some of the baseball players we didn't get to the last time. There was a funny one, a guy named Coot Veal." She stood and positioned herself by the sink. For a girl who'd grown up with maid service, Blair had adapted to the drudgery of manual dish-cleaning with remarkable ease. "Your dad's great."

"He is," Miller said. "But I didn't know you were planning on seeing him alone. I was surprised when he mentioned it."

"Was it a problem?"

"No," Miller said. He stretched some plastic wrap over the leftover rice and stuck it in the fridge, buying himself time to consider his objections. "It was just a little weird, like my dad and my girl getting together behind my back."

Blair wiped her hands on a dishrag. "My dad's never around,

you know," she said. "I think I was just craving an hour or two with a nice old guy."

"And you picked my dad?"

"Well, how many nice old guys do I know?" she said. "Besides, he's got a lot of stories to tell."

"I've got a lot of stories to tell," Miller said. He picked up a sponge and began to rub the kitchen counter free of grease. "I've got lots to tell you."

"There's no need to get competitive," she said.

"I'm not competitive," Miller lied. He stopped scrubbing and lit a cigarette. "It's just that—" He tried to find the words to explain himself. "Evidently, right before my dad and my mom split up, he was having some flings with different women. Different, you know, younger women. And maybe it happened for years, I don't know. I mean, I never asked too many questions, and he didn't tell me more than I needed to hear, but . . ."

"You've got to be kidding me." Blair took Miller's cigarette from his hands, and took a drag, standing close to him.

"Well," Miller said. He was embarrassed, but also relieved to be honest about what he feared.

Blair stubbed the cigarette out onto a dirty plate, put Miller's face in her hands, and kissed him on the mouth. "Your father seems like a father to me," she said. "Nothing else."

"Okay," Miller said, warmed by the heat of her body as she pressed herself against him.

"I wanted to talk about baseball cards," she whispered, kissing him again.

"Fine with me." Miller put his hands on her ass and drew her closer.

"Sometimes it's nice to have an old man around," Blair said, sliding her hands up under his shirt. He shuddered as her fingers tugged at his nipples. He grabbed at her T-shirt, raising it over her head.

"But now is not one of those times," he whispered.

"Now is not one of those times."

He kissed her neck and the scar on her chin, and tugged at her skirt, and grunted hoarsely when she yanked his jeans down over his hips. She cried out and bit him and they moved back and forth against the kitchen counter in Queens.

Neighborly Advice

For the fifth autumn in a row, Miller watched as his apartment grew darker earlier in the day. He had never minded the darkness of the apartment—in fact, he'd appreciated it, as it hid the grime. But now, with so much light around him in the form of Blair Carter, the darkness seemed amiss, an inappropriate accompaniment to the way that he was feeling. Worse, in the damp gray daylight, the smudges on the walls seemed ever more accusatory. Plus Harry took up a lot of space.

At the end of October, Miller indeed got his promotion at BigFunCity: he was now literary editor, and was planning his first big feature, a series celebrating books about New York: *The House of Mirth, Lou Gehrig: Pride of the Yankees, Breakfast at Tiffany's*. There was talk of linking the BigFunCity site to a whole network of regional sites, maybe even going public. Miller's earnings were now officially more than toilet paper.

On the way home from work one crisp, bright Tuesday, Miller stopped in to see Ahmed, who for the past five years had sold him cigarettes, dog food, and the occasional *Rolling Stone* from his compact sundries shop on Thirty-first. Miller liked to hear the news from Ahmed, especially concerning the future of the neighborhood. Most residents of Astoria depended on the grocer for toilet paper and cigarettes, and he was therefore knowledgeable about local immigration patterns and neighborhood gossip.

In the front of the store stood the refrigerated wall of milk, beer, soda, and ice cream. In the center, near the register, were barrels of Asian spices and boxes of chutneys and cigars. Toward the back were the racks of movies, Bollywood and otherwise. The store, as usual, felt overheated, as Ahmed was suspicious of air-conditioning, and at five thirty in the evening it was also weirdly quiet.

"So what's the word?" Miller asked as he fished through the beer selection for a six-pack of Bass.

"What do you think the word is?" Ahmed groused, stylish in a purple silk shirt and pleated pants. He was fortyish, balding, mustachioed, frowning. "Nobody's here. The word is very bad."

"What's the problem?"

"You tell me what the problem is. I saw your neighbor Mrs. Plakarides yesterday; she told me that her new Honda was stolen from right off her driveway last week. An Accord, leather interior." Ahmed knew Miller's neighbors much better than Miller did himself.

"That's a shame."

"I have thought about investing in a new security system, since security is no joke, my friend. But the alarm companies want ten thousand dollars from me, and I am not a rich man." He reached into a glass cabinet next to the register for Miller's carton of Camel Lights. "It is different here now."

"Different how?" Miller placed his six-pack on the counter and scanned the store for something else to purchase, to help out his friend Ahmed.

"Well, for one thing, my customers cannot afford it here lately, and that is one of the problems. They are going to Sunnyside. Jackson Heights. They are going to the Bronx."

"What's your theory?"

"My theory is this: in Astoria I believe we are located too close to Manhattan. So this is why the young professionals are continuing to move in. People like *you*. And you do not shop at my store. You go to Manhattan or the Pathmark on Northern Boulevard. My old customers shopped at my store."

There were patches of sweat on the neck of Ahmed's purple shirt.

"Ahmed," Miller said, "I'm shopping at your store right now." He took a jar of Major Gray's chutney and placed it on the counter beside his cigarettes and his beer.

Ahmed waved his hand dismissively. "All you young professionals, you have"—here he shuddered—"decided to *quit smoking*. You want to kill me, all of you."

"Don't worry. I promise you I will never quit smoking." Miller was sure that Ahmed had never in his life touched nicotine or alcohol. "I'll keep you in business for a long time."

"No, my friend, I am getting out of here soon. It is time to go where the money is. Maybe Florida or New Jersey. I am sick, I tell you, of all this bullshit."

"I grew up in New Jersey. There's plenty of bullshit there."

But Ahmed was already staring out his plate glass window, wiping the sweat off his forehead and muttering under his breath.

As Miller walked to his apartment it started to drizzle. The drunk who lived on the corner of Thirty-ninth Street retched into the sidewalk trash bin. Miller thought to himself that Ahmed was right, that going where the money is wasn't such a bad idea.

"But Manhattan?" Blair said to him that Saturday as they hiked through Central Park, heading toward the new Planetarium. "That's where you want to move? Boring Manhattan?"

"Boring?" Miller said. "What's boring?" He remembered coming to the Planetarium on a school trip when he was a kid, and being amazed at the consequences of gravity: On Jupiter, he'd weigh 240 pounds, but on Mercury, he'd weigh almost nothing.

"It's just . . . I mean, it's so cramped, and most of it doesn't have any of the character of Queens." Blair looked wary. "Would you even be able to afford an apartment?"

"I can find something affordable," Miller said. He paused, and then decided to hit her with his sucker punch: "And your neighborhood seems like a reasonable choice."

Blair stopped walking. She looked mystified. "Why?"

Why? he thought to himself. *Why?* He took her hand and started leading her along the trail again. *Why? Well, basically,* Miller thought, *because that's where you are, my princess, my angel, my light. Wherever you are is where I want to be all the time.* "I don't know," Miller said. "I've kind of always liked the Upper East Side."

"I didn't know that," Blair said. "I'm surprised. You don't really seem like the type."

"What's the type?" he asked.

Blair said, "Wealthier."

"I just got a promotion," he reminded her.

"More spoiled," she said. "Sillier."

"Queens is plenty silly," Miller said. "I can be silly."

"There's better food in Queens," she said.

"There's *cheaper* food in Queens," he said. "But, you know, the Upper East Side has better bookstores. Anyway, I keep telling you, I got a promotion."

"Queens has decent bookstores. And anyway, I don't think you'll like it. And if you don't, then you can't pretend I didn't warn you." She paused. "If I were you, I'd seriously consider other neighborhoods."

Miller felt a small rumble of distress in his gut. He had imagined that Blair, upon news that he was uprooting himself and moving to her neighborhood, would jump up and down with the thrill of it, or at the very least give her approval. "I'm twenty-seven," Miller said, taking his hand out of hers and putting it in his pocket. "I'm too old to live in a basement."

He sat down on an ornate green bench near the reservoir. Blair passed him a bottle of water from her backpack and then sat next to him, her hand casually landing on his leg. She had short fingers and straight pink nails, polished at her standing twice-weekly appointment. These were the sort of nails that Miller's mother strove for and could never achieve, what with her picking and biting.

"Well, maybe you'll find some good space," Blair said. "There are cheaper apartments north of Ninety-sixth Street. But I still think there are better neighborhoods for you to live in. Maybe the Lower East Side," she said. "Or even Brooklyn."

"I'm not interested in Brooklyn." Miller was torn between enjoying the feel of Blair's hand on his leg and the irritation beginning to chew at him.

"Okay," Blair said, in a reasonable tone of voice. "Whatever." She took her hand off Miller's leg and wrapped her red woolen scarf tighter around her neck. In the autumn light, Blair looked like something out of an L.L. Bean catalog, blond hair gleaming against knit scarf, brown corduroy coat buttoned halfway, off-white cabled fisherman's sweater meeting the scarf at her throat. Her bright blue eyes and her bright white teeth were almost comically perfect. Miller felt a pang of resentment at how lovely she was and how little she seemed to care about his resolve to join her on the Upper East Side. Then he felt embarrassed by his resentment, but he couldn't quite shake it off. And all the while, Blair noticed nothing. Those bright blue eyes were so blind!

"Blair," he said finally. "Don't you want me around?"

"Huh?" she said. Her eyes had been following a dalmatian puppy as he passed their way. "Of course I want you around. What are you talking about?"

"I just thought you might be happier to have me on the Upper East Side," Miller said. He stared down at his lap, knowing that he was whining, frustrated and miserable and scared that the person he was so joyfully in love with might not be as gleeful about him.

"What?" Blair said. She gazed at Miller with a mixture of amazement and indulgence. "Joel, I'd be happy to have you anywhere, as long as it was somewhere you wanted to be." She picked up his hand and kissed it. "But I don't think you should move to the Upper East Side just to be around me."

"Oh, it wouldn't be just to be near you," Miller lied. "I wasn't kidding. I like it up there. And, you know, cheap apartments north of Ninety-sixth Street."

"Okay," Blair said.

"Okay." Miller was desperate for her to kiss his hand again, or even better, to kiss his mouth. But she did not.

Having never been so wholly in love before, Miller found that it came refreshingly close to meeting most of his expectations. Yes, he woke up with a tune on his lips and a swell in his heart, and he felt that time not spent with Blair was generally wasted on waiting to be with her or remembering the last time he'd spent with her. He had started singing along with the love songs in his CD collection (Smokey Robinson's "Being With You," the Supremes' "I Hear a Symphony") and paying more attention to even the smallest wonderful things in life—freshly laundered T-shirts, half-naked girls on magazine covers.

But all this lightheartedness was matched, in some wretched respects, by an equal and opposite reaction. Miller had never felt so unworthy as he suddenly did around Blair. She was constantly making him quake. The way she cooked dinner, the way she knew her way around art, the tiny puffs she took from his cigarettes. The way she cut off the necks of her T-shirts and the way she dazzled the dog, her friends, Stanley. The things that he knew and admired about her—they couldn't help but force Miller to wonder what she could possibly know and admire about him. He started cataloging his own faults, large and small, physical and emotional. He was, he felt, unlovable in many respects. He had a secret weakness for bad music: Air Supply, Hall & Oates. There was a weird ivylike growth of hair slowly creeping over his shoulders and threatening to snake down his back. He spilled food when he was eating.

He chain-smoked. Even with his promotion, he didn't make a lot of money. He probably never would.

Some of these things Miller began to fixate on and try to improve: a week ago he found himself twisted in front of the bathroom mirror with a tweezer, attempting to denude himself of the fresh ambush of hairs aiming for his shoulders. He hid his Hall & Oates CDs. He thought about how he could make a few extra bucks, maybe do some freelancing, treat Blair in the exemplary fashion to which she was accustomed. But in the end, he feared it would be futile. He would always be himself, Joel J. Miller. And she would always be the wonderful Blair.

"I think Harry would like the Upper East Side," Blair said, generously. "You could take him for walks in the park."

"Exactly," Miller said, and leaned over to kiss her neck. "That's it exactly."

Blair picked up his hand again, and together they started walking toward the Planetarium. She was being merciful toward him, but Miller was happy to take what he could get.

Bubbles

In Park Slope, it's 12:21, almost an hour since Miller came home with the CleanTest Pink. He is no closer to knowing if Lisa's pregnant than he was an hour ago.

"I'm stuck," Lisa calls from the other side of the bathroom door.

"Stuck how?" Miller is idling in the hallway rubbing Harry's stomach. Harry yawns with delight, lets his long tongue hang out the side of his mouth.

"I mean, I can't get out of the bath without getting my cast wet."

"Do you need a hand?"

She pauses. "Yes, Miller. That'd be nice."

Miller stands, and Harry stands too, faithful. The bathroom door is locked.

"Just pound on it a couple times," Lisa says. Miller can hear water splashing inside the tub. "You know that lock never sticks."

Miller pounds twice, but nothing happens. Harry paws at the door, leans his weight against it. Miller pounds two more times, and then he and Harry burst in triumphantly. The dog jogs up to Lisa, who is sprawled in the tub, her cast propped up on the side. He licks her face.

"Good boy." She flops Harry's ears with her hand. "That's such a good boy." Harry licks her nose, the top of her ear. She looks pretty, Miller thinks, with her hair twisted up on top of her head and the faint traces of lipstick reddening her lips. She has poured bubble bath into the tub, and the bubbles froth around her neck and breasts. Miller sits down on the side of the bathtub, next to her cast.

"Stalling, huh?"

"The pee's on the counter," Lisa says. Miller looks over, sees a half-full cup alongside a dropper and a torn page of instructions. The CleanTest Pink box is propped up behind this collection: a still life.

"You know, I could just dip the stick in for you," Miller says. "It's no problem. Here, listen." He picks up the instructions and begins reading. "It says I'm supposed to hold the strip vertically and, let's see, immerse it into the urine sample with the narrow end fully submerged—"

"Miller, stop," Lisa says. "I can do this myself."

"You nervous?" he asks, reaching over to wipe bubbles off her neck.

"No," she says. "Maybe a little."

Harry sniffs Lisa's cast and then leaves the bathroom wagging his shaggy bottom. "Your bubble bath smells good," Miller says. "Like oranges."

"Apricots." Lisa lifts a dollop of bubbles with her finger and wipes them on Miller's nose. "I guess I'm not really that nervous. Whatever happens will probably be all right."

Miller is charmed by her fatalism; he takes her hand and helps her maneuver upright, his arms around her narrow waist, bubbles sliding down her thighs and pooling around the top of her cast. He lifts her over the side of the tub and lets her balance herself against the sink. Then he hands her her tattered pink bathrobe and helps her into it, as though it were a fur coat and they were leaving for a night at the opera.

"You need a new bathrobe," he says, kissing the back of her neck. "This one's a mess."

"Let me finish with the test and then I'll think about bathrobes." Lisa reaches for one of her crutches.

"Do you want me to stay here?" Unexpectedly, he hopes that she will, that she does. "I'd be happy to stay if you want." What he should say to her: I can be here for you, I can hold your hand while you take the test, I know how to be a stand-up guy, you looked pretty in the bathtub. But Lisa is already frowning past him, at her reflection in the mirror behind the sink. Frowning, and her prettiness drains away.

"Actually," she says, "I think I'd still like my privacy, if you don't mind."

"You sure?" Miller says.

"I'm sure." She lets her hair out of its clip, and it falls limply past her shoulders. "Thanks for helping me out of the tub."

"Of course."

When he leaves, he can hear her lock the door once more behind him, a silly twist of a defective lock. He thinks to himself that he should tell her not to bother, but he says nothing.

Housewarming

Grant had billed his housewarming party as a "Come as You Are"; Miller came in an old T-shirt and felt like a jackass. The men at Grant's party were wearing charcoal sweaters or neat white button-downs and sharply creased pants. "Didn't I just give you all that stuff from Barneys?" Grant said. "This is a housewarming, not a frat party." Grant himself was wearing a tan, a guayabera, and a bit of stubble: the tropical look.

On long low tables at the sides of the room were piles of exotic fruits, chicken and shrimp satays, prosciutto-wrapped slices of melon, steak tartare. There was icy vodka and caviar. The bartender poured sake and Glenlivet and Cristal.

The new loft was near the Odeon restaurant and not too far from where JFK Jr. had lived; tonight it was filled with Grant's superiors from work, a few people in the arts, and one or two who made their living from cultivating airs of mystery. Rachel was conducting the scene with a careful hand, coordinating conversation clusters and periodically feeding Grant black pearls of caviar from a small white spoon.

With little on the walls, and lighting that seemed to emanate from nowhere, the loft was cavernous. People stood backlit, like individual pieces of installation art. Miller scanned their faces, looking for anyone who seemed familiar, but there was no one. He felt shabby, clumsy, unable to make small talk, and would have left were he not waiting for Blair. Just then he noticed that the line for the bathroom was eight people long, a good way to stall until she arrived.

"So, who do you know?" said the woman in front of him. She was wearing leather pants and a sparkly T-shirt, and her lipstick was the deep red of mistletoe.

"Me?" Miller said. "Oh, nobody, really." Technically, a lie: he could see his old friend Grant across the room, talking to two men with shaved heads.

The girl flipped her hair off her face with an extravagant motion. "Me neither," she said. "I mean, I came to this party with a friend from work but she just ditched me to go home with this banker. I was like, nine P.M. is a little soon to go home with someone, but she was just like, shut up. I think she and the banker guy were both high or something, I don't know. They were so hyper." The girl flipped her hair again. "They were in this bathroom together for a really long time. Hence the backup."

"Seems impolite."

"Oh, totally. But what do you expect at this sort of party?" The girl shrugged. "My friend was all, maybe we'll meet some venture capitalists and we can quit our stupid day jobs. Or at least get laid."

"Well, her plan was sort of successful, then."

"You're not a venture capitalist, huh?"

"Sorry," Miller said.

"Oh, that's okay. I told my friend, I was like, I don't care what a guy does or how much money he makes, not really, as long as he doesn't treat me like shit."

"You should have higher standards."

The girl smiled, bit the corner of her fingernail. "I know," she said. "But it can be hard in this city."

"I know what you mean."

He could remember once, a few years earlier, when a woman like this would have filled him with a sense of possibility. She was young, sure, and her conversation was ridiculous; but on the other hand, in a different environment (at work, at the Laundromat, on the phone with her mother) it was possible that she was smarter, less fidgety. Moreover, she was pretty, and at this very moment she was alone in the world. Miller often felt comfortable with loners.

The girl seemed to sense that she was being assessed; she stood straighter and reapplied her lipstick. Miller lit a cigarette and offered her one.

"Oh, sure, thanks," she said, and puffed on it inexpertly. "So what's your name, anyway?"

"I'm Miller."

"Just Miller? That's funny. Oh, look, the bathroom's free."

"Go ahead," Miller said.

"You sure? Guys don't take as long, so if you want you can go first."

"You first," Miller said chivalrously. "I insist."

"But will you still be here when I get out?"

She didn't wait for an answer, and as soon as the door was closed he ducked out of the bathroom line and headed for the bar. It was almost ten o'clock. All right already. Where was Blair?

A ringing from the center of the room, a fork on crystal, a clear high-pitched ping. The music stopped immediately.

"Excuse me," Grant said. "Ladies and gentlemen, honored friends and guests." He was standing in the middle of his brand-new loft, encircled by a few feet of empty space, holding a fork in one hand and a goblet in the other. "Excuse me, ladies and gentlemen, your attention, please." He was sweating. His cheeks were red. Miller wondered if his friend was high.

"First of all, I wanted to thank you all for joining me this evening." *Hear! Hear!* was called from someone in the corner. "It's a privilege and an honor—no, an *honor* and a *privilege*—to welcome you all to my new home."

Grant swayed for a second but then steadied himself. Miller pushed his way through the group that surrounded his friend. He hoped Grant was okay. "Second of all," Grant said, "I wanted to thank the woman who makes it all happen, the woman who inspires me, the woman who makes me excited to wake up in the morning. The most beautiful woman in the world. Rachel, baby, I love you."

All eyes shifted to Rachel, whose lips were pressed together in a not altogether pleased expression. "True love!" shrieked someone in the crowd.

"And thirdly, because you are all my friends, and because Rachel is the woman I love, and because . . . well, what the hell." And with this, Grant, still bearing the goblet and the fork, got down on one knee and smiled hopefully up at the crowd. Someone pushed Rachel forward. "Marry me, Rachel Jones," Grant said.

"Oh, my God," Rachel said.

"Marry me," Grant repeated.

"Marry him!" heckled a guest.

"Stand up, you idiot," Rachel said to the man on his knee before her. Grant put down the goblet and the fork, and stood up, and Rachel whispered something in his ear, and then Grant treated her to a long, openmouthed kiss. The crowd cheered. The music came back on.

"I wonder what she said to him," said a familiar voice to Miller's left. Blair.

"From the way they're smooching," Miller said, "I'm guessing she said yes."

Blair nodded. Miller was delighted. Grant was getting married, it was suddenly a beautiful evening, and his own lovely Blair had just arrived. He bent down and kissed his lady hello, as extravagantly as Grant was kissing Rachel just a few feet away.

Confession

The party had taken on a certain schmaltziness after Grant's proposal; someone had switched the music to Dean Martin, and Grant and Rachel twirled around the hardwood floors of the loft in a modified swing. The bar was running out of tonic and Miller and Blair offered to retrieve some from the kitchen for one of the overworked bartenders.

"A proposal," Blair said. "Can you believe that? Can you believe it?"

"Well, they've been together for a while." Grant's kitchen

was small and white, with an enormous refrigerator and microwave but a tiny stove. Dean Martin pumped in through the thin door.

"But I've got to admit I'm surprised," Blair said. "Grant didn't seem like the marrying kind."

"What's the marrying kind?"

"Guys who seem committed to one thing at a time. Guys who don't live in Tribeca. Not Grant."

"Not Grant," Miller said, "until he found Rachel." *Not me*, he thought, *until I found you.* A woman, a stranger, stuck her head in the kitchen and then retreated and, once she did, it struck Miller that he and his girl were enviably alone.

"I love you," he whispered hoarsely. The thought flew out of his mouth like a nervous bird. Blair turned to dig through the ice container in the refrigerator. She did not respond.

"I love you," he said again, slightly louder.

"What?" Blair said. "It's noisy in here."

"I love you," Miller said a third time, but as he did someone outside turned up the music and Dean Martin's voice drowned out his words.

"What?" Blair said again.

This was becoming embarrassing. "Oh," he said. "Just—nothing." And he picked up two large bottles of tonic from the counter and followed Blair back into the party. His heart was beating fast. Blair, delicate and lovely in her blue dress, was instantly surrounded by people who seemed to know her. Miller slunk out behind, depleted from the failed attempt to declare his love. He was hoping that she really hadn't heard him, for he couldn't bear to think that she had preferred not to respond.

Of course, you already knew that this would happen.

New Digs

And then conditions became worrisome. When the time came, Blair refused to help him look for an apartment. "I've got things to do."

"You don't have anything to do," Miller countered. "What do you have to do?"

"My father," she explained, and as far as she was concerned, that was enough. It had been six months now and still the closest Miller had come to meeting Reynold Carter was a voyage through his baseball card collection. In Miller's mind, however, the man had started to assume the dimensions of an ancient god: demanding, omnipotent, capricious. Reynold would disappear for weeks at a time—he seemed particularly fond of executive meetings in Vienna—but then he'd reappear, without warning, and require all of Blair's time for days in a row.

"It's just a couple hours with a broker," Miller said. "Couldn't you ditch him for just a few hours?"

"Joel," Blair said, her voice hushed on the phone, "you know I can't."

"I don't understand," Miller said, but that was untrue. Miller did understand, because if he had Blair around whenever he wanted, he wouldn't want to let her go either.

So on a cloudy Saturday morning in November, Miller grabbed Jed Hilary, the office jackal. Jed was the right choice for an Upper East Side apartment search; his BigFunCity beat was, in fact, the Upper East Side, and, further, he was currently sleeping with the real estate agent who had helped him land a one-bedroom on York Avenue.

"You want north," Jed said, forking eggs into his mouth. At thirty, Jed was balding and his face already hinted at what he would look like in twenty years. Scrawny in an oversize polo shirt, with thin loose curls sprouting around a bald patch, he laughed with a rasping sound. He ate his eggs gracelessly. "I mean, what you really want is south, but let's face it, you're not making south money and you probably never will. So north is what you want. But maybe near the park?"

"I want a new zip code," Miller said.

"And a new zip code," Jed said, pointing his egg-laden fork at Miller, "is what you shall have. But I've been doing the BigFun rental price review, and let me tell you, friend, it's ugly out there." Jed slathered up a piece of toast with some jam and took a bite out of it that left perfect perforation marks in the shape of his teeth.

Melinda Chen, Jed's little piece of personal real estate, picked them up a few minutes later at the diner on Eighty-fourth with a business card and a clipboard. "I've got something on Ninety-seventh that you can afford," she said to Miller, instead of "nice to meet you." "Pay for your coffee. Let's get a move on."

"Hiya, baby," Jed said. He pulled her down into the booth next to him and kissed her on the cheek.

Melinda sighed as though she had no time to waste being kissed. She was pretty, Miller thought, even in her severe gray blazer. Her thick black hair was twisted neatly at her neck. "It's a tough market out there," Melinda said. "Everyone wants this apartment. I don't have an exclusive. It'll be gone in an hour. Monkey business later." Jed nibbled on her ear. "Let's go let's go let's go." Miller thought she sounded like a field-hockey coach.

The apartment was on Ninety-seventh Street off Lexington Avenue, on a schizophrenic block near several bars and the largest mosque in Manhattan. Two rooms in a plain brick building with dusty tiled floors and a grimy mosaic in the lobby, a broken intercom system, and a row of gray metal mailboxes lining the first-floor hall. Melinda led them up three flights of stairs, and Jed grabbed at her ass several times per flight.

"Here we are," Melinda said, after fumbling with the top key and then the bottom and then the top one again. "We beat the crowds."

Two rooms, small but smelling of fresh paint; wood floors, a closet, and another closet, which upon closer inspection turned out to be the kitchen. There was a mini-fridge and a two-burner stove. "How much?" Miller asked.

"Less than you would have guessed," Melinda said smoothly. "The landlord lives in Florida. He hasn't been keeping up on rental prices."

The bathroom had a plastic shower compartment, a cracked vanity, and cheap chrome hardware. In a normal city, the amount of rent the landlord required would seem either laughable or criminal, but in this town the price tag on the apartment was, if not a bargain, certainly within reason. Miller knew it, and although he had inherited his mother's dream of doormen with peaked caps, he wanted to move and he was no fool.

"I'll take it," he said.

"Bravo," Melinda said, and Jed kissed her again, to celebrate.

Deluxe Apartments in the Sky

Miller rented a mini U-Haul with a picture of crayfish and VISIT LOUISIANA! written on the side in orange script and loaded cartons of books, a box of CDs, an old plastic trash can full of dishes and clothes. Grant helped him lift his heavier items into the U-Haul: the futon, the bookshelf, the dresser, the dog.

"I see so many possibilities," Rachel said. She was standing goddesslike on the boxes, reaching up toward the ceiling to remove the cracked shade that guarded the living room's main source of light. She was an inch taller than Grant and more dexterous, she believed, than Miller. Her shirt rose as she unscrewed, revealing new, lacy tattoos across her stomach.

"What kind of possibilities?"

"Paint the walls, first of all. What color do you have right now, China white?"

"I have no idea," Miller said. Frankly, to him it was enough that the paint on the walls was new.

"It's definitely China white. That's the bullshit landlord standard. It's like a default color. You can do so much better."

"Rachel has an excellent eye for color," Grant said.

"Maybe something like a saffron. Saffron's a lovely color for walls." Her British accent made the word *saffron* luxurious.

"I have no idea what color saffron is," Miller admitted.

"It's yellow, you philistine," Grant said.

"It's like a very refined yellow," Rachel said. "It's like a sort of Moroccan shade."

"Moroccan yellow?"

"Saffron," Rachel said. "We should order in dinner, by the way. All this housework has left me properly famished."

Grant leaned against a box of books and tapped his cigarette into a can of Coke. "You know, six more months, I could have given you the loft." He and Rachel were planning on getting married in her father's hometown in Jamaica and then boating around the world. The brand-new loft, pride of Grant's recent history, was going to be sublet. He would take a leave of absence from his job.

"I didn't want to wait six months," Miller said.

"He wanted to be near Blair," Rachel said, and Miller did not protest. Shade successfully removed, Rachel sat down cross-legged next to Grant and Miller and took a Camel Light from Miller's pack.

Harry shuffled up next to the three on the floor and sniffed each of them, then plopped down next to his owner, a sign of fidelity that Miller found reassuring. He felt, on the floor of his new apartment, that everything was coming into its rightful place. He scratched Harry behind the ears.

Tremors

Three mornings later Rachel woke Grant, her fiancé of twenty-six days, by kissing him on the shoulders and neck. "I can't marry you," she said. "This isn't working for me."

Grant rolled over and looked at the clock. It was eight thirty in the morning and Rachel, the woman with whom he had planned on spending his life, was naked in bed next to him. But she was already sitting up, looking around for her underwear.

"Get out, then," Grant said, too shocked to be anything but cruel.

She did, her spaghetti legs shrugging into jeans, her hair wedged under a newsboy cap. She closed the door behind her when she left.

"And that was it?" Miller asked. Later they sat at a bar on Ninety-first Street, an Irish joint with posters from last year's Super Bowl blocking out the light from the windows. It was two in the afternoon, a Sunday.

Grant, hungry-looking and unshaven, tossed down the last of his Dewar's. "She can't deal with commitment. She's not ready to settle down." He shrugged, and signaled for more booze. "What can you do?"

They stayed at the bar until the bar wouldn't let them stay any longer, and then Miller took Grant to his own new apartment, where most of the furniture was still in boxes, and put him to bed on his futon. Miller himself took the floor.

• • •

And he wanted to ask Blair why Rachel might have done it, might so casually have broken his best friend's heart. But he thought Blair might have too obvious an answer or know too well how a woman can just get up and leave. Or he thought that maybe questioning Rachel's flight would make Blair think about flying away herself.

"Is Grant okay?" she asked on the phone the next night.

"No," Miller said. "But he will be."

"Of course he *will* be," Blair said.

"Why of course?"

"Oh," Blair said. He could hear her draw in on a cigarette. "Grant seems like the resilient type," she said.

"He's not resilient," Miller said. "He's drunk. You shouldn't be smoking."

"I hate you for getting me addicted to this," she snapped. Miller winced. Quickly her tone changed. "Look, not to make light of it or anything, but there are worse tragedies. Grant will fall in love again with someone else, and eventually he'll love that someone else more, and he'll be grateful for the rest of his life that Rachel did what she did."

"I guess," Miller said, although he didn't quite believe it.

"Trust me," Blair said, before saying good night and hanging up the phone.

Park City

So there had been signs. Miller had been forewarned. And frankly, if he hadn't been concentrating on home furnishings that afternoon, he might have seen it coming. But instead Miller was standing in the corner of the living room with an Ikea catalog in one hand and a tape measure in the other. He was putting more thought than ever before into the subject of couches, weighing the "Falsterbo," a convertible model, against the pricier but more stylish "Göteborg."

Blair was due to come over—her first official visit to his new apartment—and he wanted to help her imagine what it would look like with furniture. The Göteborg couch, almost certainly. With the Hallum coffee table and the Leksvik bookshelf against the wall. The Granat cushion for Harry to sleep on. Although he was disappointed by how long it had taken her to come visit—it had been a full week since they'd seen each other—he was already half-erect from the idea of kicking aside the boxes and fucking her on his new hardwood floors.

She arrived three minutes early—he still loved how she was always early—and he pushed her against the wall of his apartment and began kissing her neck with an urgency brought on by their separation and the domesticity of combing through an Ikea catalog for hours alone. He smelled her soapy, grassy smell, licked the scar on her chin, kissed her ear and the tops of her shoulders. He was not dissuaded by her lack of responsiveness, because he was too caught up in his own excitement to notice.

"Joel," she said.

"Mmm, Blair," he said, tugging at the buttons of her blouse.

"Joel," she said again, more firmly, putting a hand on his chest. She wiggled out from between Miller and the wall, and wiped some of his saliva off her cheek.

He felt his hard-on wither. "What's wrong?"

"I need to talk to you," she said.

Looking back on this day, as he would for weeks and months and years later, Miller knew that the "I need to talk" line should have been as sure a warning signal as a lighthouse beaming from the shore, but still he was too giddy with his apartment and her presence to take notice.

"Okay," he said. He wiped his hands on his jeans and lit a Camel Light, watching her examine his new apartment with the same care with which she had first inspected his Queens basement six months earlier. "What do you need to talk to me about?" He took an almost empty can of Diet Sprite from the top of a box and tapped the ash from his cigarette into it.

"I'm leaving," Blair said.

"Excuse me?"

"I'm leaving." She was still examining the walls of his apartment, the moldings around the doors. She ran her finger around a doorknob.

"I don't get it."

"I'm leaving," she said. "I'm going away. Alone."

"I don't understand." Where could she be going? He had just found this apartment, twenty-seven blocks north of her own on the Upper East Side. He wasn't going anywhere, so how could she be leaving?

"I'm sorry," she said.

Miller pressed himself into the corner of the living room, near the kitchen. He thought: *If I press myself into this wall, if I push myself through the wall, if I break the time-space continuum right here in this apartment, this will not be happening. It will never have happened.* "Well, where are you going?" he asked, voice beginning to break.

"I've been thinking," Blair said, "about Park City."

Park City? Miller scrolled through the database of his memory, searching for a Park City reference in his conversations with Blair. Park City, Park City—that was Utah, wasn't it? Or Colorado? Where the hell was Park City? How could she be saying this?

Blair shrugged her shoulders. She sat down on his new floor, leaned against his new wall, and Miller already knew that he would have to find a different apartment. Outside, an ambulance wailed.

"What the fuck," he asked, "is in Park City?"

"What's with your tone?"

"What's in Park City?"

"Pine trees. Mountains. I can ski."

"That's not a reason to move. That's not a reason to leave here."

"I'm tired of New York, Joel." She drew her knees to her chest.

"You're tired of New York?" he asked. How on earth could that be possible? Miller sat down opposite her on an unpacked carton of records and tried to get her to look him in the eye. "But I'm in New York."

He thought, *If she just looks at me, if she just looks at my face, then she will have to change her mind. She cannot leave me if she just looks at me.*

Blair stared at the box that Miller was using as a chair.

"This is not what you're supposed to do," Miller said, catching on to the desperation in his voice only after it was too late. "You can't leave. Please don't go to Park City, it isn't right. I've never even heard you *talk* about Park City before; I've never even heard you mention it. . . . You can't—" Miller felt his breath speed up, his heart speed up, and without warning he remembered losing his mother in a supermarket when he was four and being sure he'd never see her again. He remembered thinking that he might as well curl up under the Dumpster in the parking lot and die. "Blair," Miller said.

"This is not where I want to live anymore," she said gently. He wished she would touch him while she tried to explain. *If she touches me*, he thought. *If she looks at me* . . . "This is not where my opportunities are. I've been in New York City most of my life. There's nothing left here for me," she said.

"I'm here," Miller said.

"I know."

The silence in the room was like loud music, oppressive and clumsy. Miller thought he could hear the actual beat in his ears, but then he realized that it was the blood coursing through them. He was doing what he could not to yell. Blair had slung an arm over her eyes, but he didn't see tears running down her cheeks.

"When did you decide this?" he finally asked. "To leave?" He stood up and went to the bookcase and dug out a new pack of cigarettes. He lit one and opened the window, stunned at how unforgiving, unforgivable she was. She was leaving him in his brand-new apartment, alone.

Blair didn't respond. She got up, touched him on the waist for a second, and then she sat back down where she had been. "I guess when I knew that you loved me too much."

"Oh," Miller said. "When I loved you too much." He blew a stream of smoke into the room, wanting to fill her with it, wanting to spray cancer into her lungs. "And what exactly is too much?"

Blair gazed at the carpet. This was when she started to cry, but prettily, tears painting patterns down her pink cheeks, round blue eyes shiny. "Too much," she said, "is more than I'll ever love you." But even this she said dully, like she was listing ingredients from the back of a cereal box.

Miller threw his cigarette out the open window, went into the bedroom, sat down on the floor, and gave up. Pain ripped him open like knives.

• • •

At midnight, Miller walked Harry to the bodega. He bought three six-packs, a carton of cigarettes, and a box of aspirin. At four in the morning, on his third pack of Camel Lights and his ninth can of Coors, Miller dragged his laptop out of a box and typed out a list:

How to Get Blair Back: In No Particular Order

1. **Kidnap** her, **Lindbergh baby–style.**
2. Tell everyone I know & also everyone who knows her & also everyone who knows us together that she's making **the biggest mistake of her life**. Provide backup documentation: photos of us together, **every message she ever left me (ESP. HORNY ONES);** distribute. Use: Grant, my father. Her doorman. Find way to get in touch with Rachel (explain to Grant: emergency). Ask **Rachel** to plead my case.
3. Leave **dog Harry** on her doorstep. Blair loves Harry.
4. Show up at apartment and beg: tell her nobody else will ever love her this much again. Remember to comb hair and not smoke too much before arrival; **STAY**

CUTE. But: how to get past doorman? (Convince doorman I'm still allowed upstairs. Use: bribery, man-to-man confidences, threats.)

5. **Hope for her father's death.** Blair loves father. Only constant in Blair's life = father. **Without father, she has no center, needs: me.** But: Wait for father to die by natural methods? Arrange nonviolent accidental death? How? Ask: Grant, Jed Hilary, consult Internet.

•

At four twenty-nine in the morning, Miller was out of ideas. He pressed SAVE. Then he lay down next to Harry and read the items on his list again and again, staring at the laptop screen and squinting his eyes. Slowly he felt his mind clear with drunken practicality.

Number one on the list was illegal. Number two was idiotic, and number three unfair to Harry. Number four was also idiotic and also possibly illegal.

But number five.

Number five was different because it didn't require Miller to actually *do* anything, or at least to do anything obvious to Blair. That was the trick: to get Blair to come back of her own accord. To go about his business in a day-to-day fashion and wait for her to come back, and to make it inevitable that she *would* come back.

Miller thought: upon learning of Reynold's death, Blair would be so distraught that she'd have no choice but to automatically return to him. She'd have no choice, running into the arms of the only man left on the planet who loved her, the only man left who would take care of her, who would protect her from the world. Also, without her father to demand all her time, Blair would finally feel like a free woman. She could stay in New York and maintain her liberty. She wouldn't need to indulge this insane and destructive fantasy about fucking Park City.

Park City?

Although not a violent man by nature, Miller felt that killing Blair's father was a necessary sacrifice for the greater good. He wondered whether or not Reynold Carter was healthy—sure, he looked fit in that photo in the Hamptons, but perhaps the years had taken a toll on him. He wondered how the man's heart was holding up. He wondered if there was any practical way to sabotage Reynold's diet or push him in front of a train.

He'd think more on it tomorrow. Comforted by a plan of action, Miller fell asleep.

• • •

The next morning, in the first second his eyes were open, Miller did not remember. Then he did. Blair was gone; she had left him; he was alone in an unsteady and miserable world. In the dim light of his hangover, killing Reynold Carter did not seem like a suitable solution. Miller needed something else. He had to fix this.

"Unpack," he said out loud.

Unpack, and scrub the kitchen, and buy some chairs, and breathe out. There was nothing else he could think of to do.

Instead, the phone rang.

There was a stranger on the phone.

The stranger confirmed that she was speaking to Miller, and then apologized.

The stranger was a waitress. She told Miller that his father had suffered a heart attack that morning, while drinking his morning coffee. His father, Stanley, had not survived.

Blair was no longer a subject of any importance.

Miller thought to himself, hungover and still disbelieving, that this was a solution to the problem of Blair Carter that had certainly never come to mind.

Quickly

Stan died at the diner, drinking his morning coffee.

In some ways, his death was better than it could have been. He was not alone, and he went quickly. At nine fifteen a minor heart attack had him on the floor, holding his chest, asking the nervous waitress to call an ambulance. She complied. Stan then asked her to call his son, Joel, at his new apartment. The number was in Stan's electronic organizer, which he managed to hold out to the waitress. But then a second heart attack, and this one was massive; Stan's eyes rolled and his lips peeled back in anguish. The waitress screamed. She could not figure out how to work the electronic organizer. Another waitress helped her find Miller's number, but it took a while, and Miller only received the phone call after the ambulance arrived to take Stan's warm, heavy body away.

Bay

Bay arrived after midnight and found her son on the floor of his apartment, staring at the ceiling. They had not seen each other in five years.

The door to the apartment had remained unlocked since Blair had walked out the night before. "Joel," she said softly.

"Mom," Miller said. "You're here."

"Of course."

Bay put down her suitcase, lay down on the floor next to her only child, and held him in her arms.

"I'm so sorry," she said finally. The moon was full over Ninety-seventh Street, and its light shined in through the open, curtainless window. Miller was wearing the same T-shirt he'd been wearing for the past two days, sweat gluing it to his armpits and his chest. He could smell himself, but he could also smell the peachy scent of his mother. She was still wearing the same perfume she had worn throughout his childhood, a drugstore brand sold in a plastic fruit-shaped bottle.

"I'm sorry too, mom." Miller sat up and ran his hands through his hair. It felt silky with grime.

Bay sat up. She was focused intently on the floor next to Miller. A pack of Camel Lights. "Do you mind?" she asked.

"You really shouldn't," Miller said, extracting a cigarette from the pack. He tossed it to her, and lit one for himself.

Bay rolled the cigarette in between two fingers. "That's lovely," she said, after her first drag. "That's really the best."

"I know," Miller said.

"It almost makes me feel better."

"Almost." Miller looked at the bright light on the floor, the silver glow from the moon. "I lost my girl yesterday, mom. Can you believe it? All this, and I lost my girl, too." Bay was watching the smoke from her cigarette float up toward the ceiling.

"Well," she said, "I guess I know how you feel."

Wanderer

They took Stan's ashes through New Jersey, driving his Cadillac down the turnpike in silence. Bay drove with more assurance than Miller would have expected. She looked good, he thought, her hair short and neat, her face smooth. She was dressed in a dark pantsuit and a white T-shirt underneath. There were pearls in her ears. She didn't wear lipstick, but periodically she'd pull some ChapStick out of her pocket and spread it carefully on her lips.

New Jersey whizzed by in smokestacks and service lanes, blighted wetlands made even more anemic by their proximity to the factories. A Liz Claiborne warehouse, an Ikea warehouse, signs for Newark Airport, the Meadowlands. A heron standing straight in the weedy reeds that lined the highway.

Miller pressed his head against the window. All the men in passing cars looked like his father.

My father is dead right now, Miller thought.

My father, who loved beer and pretty girls and big cars and baseball games, is dead.

My father, who loved his Cadillac, loved to eat salsa, loved to schmooze the doctors.

My father, who didn't know much about a lot of things, but who knew enough to get by almost anywhere—my father, who could hold his own on the golf course, if he needed to. He knew about art. He owned a pair of calfskin gloves.

He didn't need those calfskin gloves, now that he was dead. He didn't need his gloves and he didn't need his baseball cards and I should have loved him better, I should have spent more time with him, I should have recognized that he was lonely and made it my business to make him less lonely, to be his friend. My father loved people, and my father loved me. I was selfish and suspicious. I was not the son he deserved.

Miller wiped his nose on his sleeve and blotted at his eyes with his forefinger and his thumb. All day Sunday he had lain on the floor, not crying, not moving. And he wouldn't let himself cry now, either. It seemed like the wrong thing to do. When he was a kid, his father hated to watch him cry.

"It's his own damn fault," Bay said, after they passed the exit for Elizabeth.

"What?" Miller said, surprised to find himself in this car, his father's car, with his mother. He kept being surprised at the fact of it, that his father was dead, that he no longer had a father, and that Bay was here.

"Stan loved to eat all that fried crap, french fries."

"I guess," Miller mumbled.

"And hot dogs."

They were silent. Then Bay said, "And pie. Jesus, how that man loved to eat a piece of pie." Sighing, she punched a button on the Cadillac's dashboard tape deck. The car was suddenly flooded with one of his old favorites, Dion singing "Wanderer."

Oh yeah, I'm the type of guy that likes to roam around,
I'm never in one place, I roam from town to town.

And then Bay joined in in her surprisingly high and pretty voice:

"And when I find myself a-fallin' for some girl
I hop right into that car of mine
Drive around the world
'Cause I'm a wanderer, yeah a wanderer
I roam around-around-around-around-around
'Cause I'm a wanderer, yeah a wanderer
I roam around-around-around-around-around."

Planes took off from Newark Airport and flew overhead, alarmingly close to the ground. "He loved you," Bay said.

"Don't, mom."

"It's important that you know it," Bay said. "He loved you very very much."

"This is something I'd rather not talk about."

"You're just like him, you know. Quiet all the time, and then you're dead."

Bay had been remarkably efficient for the past three days, dealing with the coroner, the lawyer, the funeral home; deciding to cremate Stanley, deciding what to do with his ashes, calling his few distant relatives and letting them know. During all this activity she remained calm—she no longer seemed to shriek or lose her temper. She chewed lots of Trident and, like Miller, never cried.

"He loved you too," Miller said. He wasn't sure whether or not she wanted to hear it, but he knew it was true.

The tape shut off with a click. Bay took Miller's hand from across the long velvety seat of the Cadillac and squeezed it, hard. "I think you're right," she said.

"He did, he loved you."

"Sometimes I thought he didn't."

"But he always did."

"I think you're right," Bay said again.

Gulls

Two hours later they found the boardwalk in Ocean City, New Jersey. In the winter, the Jersey shore is an oily study in gray: the white-tipped gray of the ocean, the sullen pale gray of the skies. And the few people who stick around during the off-season, ghosts of the summer, all have peculiar complexions, bleached an ironic gray after too many Augusts in the sun.

They parked in the deserted lot in front of Crabby Jerry's Seafood House and cut their way around the restaurant, picking careful footsteps over desiccated buoys and crab carapaces. Seagulls, sensing humans and the possibility of food, chattered and swooped and shrieked above their heads. Without thinking, Miller took his mother's hand. They found the stairs behind the restaurant that led to the boardwalk and climbed them in silence.

Bay held Stan's ashes in a white porcelain jar. They carried them past the metal screens that guarded the shoot-the-duck, dunk-the-monkey, win-the-toy games from the erosions of winter. A faint scent of popcorn lingered in their noses, along with a saccharine whiff of coconut lotion and the bloody, salty smell of the ocean.

Past the bandstand and the hot dog stand, past the changing cabanas and a lineup of corroding Portosans, they arrived at the pier. Bay let go of Miller's hand and held the porcelain jar close against her chest. It was not particularly windy, but the air held a bite of late autumn cold. They walked the length of the pier while the seagulls screamed from their perches.

By the time they reached the end of the pier, Bay's eyes were red and her nose was running, but Miller was afraid to do anything besides quickly touch her shoulder. He didn't know how he would hold up if she started to cry.

Bay closed her eyes tightly and then opened them, turning to face the water. She unscrewed the lid of the porcelain jar, letting Stan's ashes blow away, into the air, and then the sea.

"So that's it?"

"I guess that's it," Miller said.

They stood quietly watching the ocean. Bay said, "Goodbye, Stanley."

The seagulls cried and flew into the wind. Beneath them, the ocean churned like it was boiling.

China

They were in a cab to LaGuardia. Bay was going home.

At the airport, an hour early for her flight, she bought the *New York Times* and a box of Tylenol PM. "First drugs I've taken in quite some time," she said. "Don't tell my doctors." In the end, it was California—sunshine, good food, homeopathy, and distance—that seemed to have cured her.

"Will you be okay?"

"Sure," she said. "But I've been away too long. I'd like to come back and see you soon. Or you could come visit me—I'm just your mother, you know. I don't bite."

Bay had spent these last years managing a dentist's office, living down the street from her sister, and seeing a therapist three times a week. It had seemed such a small, sad life, and Miller had not wanted to know about it. But now he knew better. "I will," he said. "I'll come soon."

They were standing together in the terminal. It seemed like someone should say something else, but neither one of them was up to the challenge. Instead they poked through the magazine kiosk. Once in a while they'd touch each other's hands, but furtively, as Miller walked her to the security screening.

"Thanks for coming to the airport," Bay said. "It was silly, you know. You didn't have to."

"I wanted to," Miller said. He thought to himself: *When she leaves I'll have nobody left in the world*. But then he thought that maybe there was some relief in that.

"I'm glad you did," Bay said. "I mean, you didn't have to, but it was nice." Miller's mother, lined by years of being sad and crazy, seemed rather beautiful to Miller, even under the harsh fluorescent lights of LaGuardia Airport.

"He was the Mao to my China," she said quietly. "Loving your father was the story of my life." Then she kissed Miller on the forehead, and then on the cheek, and then she squeezed his hands again, and then she got on the plane.

Orphans

Two weeks later, Miller still had not unpacked. He was living among the boxes, which he treated as furniture. When he got dressed, he pulled clothes out of a box marked CLOTHES & ETC. When he ate, he ate off the box that contained cookware. He did not have guests and did not expect any. So, on the Sunday evening precisely two weeks after Stan died, Miller was jolted by the sound of the doorbell.

It was Blair, standing on the doormat, wearing jeans, a heavy sweater, gloves.

He could not speak.

She cleared her throat. "I heard about your father," she said. "I'm sorry."

"Oh." He felt good manners tug at him; he should step aside, let her through the door, but he was paralyzed by the adrenaline pulsing through his body. When the doorbell rang, he'd assumed it was a lost visitor, someone in search of someone else. But now here she was. Two weeks gone from his life and already as absent as God. He had forgotten how short she was.

"I wanted to tell you how much I liked him," she said to the floor. "I thought he was great."

"He was great," Miller said.

"Of course he was, of course, you didn't need me to tell you that. But I know what it's like to lose a father, how lonely it is, and I . . ." She trailed off.

"You know what it's like to lose a father?" Miller asked, stunned at the nerve of it, of her comparing a father who merely traveled a lot to one who was dead and gone.

"I know what it's like," Blair repeated, and looked up. "My own father died when I was eighteen," she said. "I miss him all the time."

It took a moment for Miller to understand her. "Your own father—"

"He's been dead for a long time," Blair said. "I just kind of don't talk about it. He's not entirely dead to me, you know. I still live in his house, I live with his things."

"Your father's dead?"

"Yes."

"You lied about the fact that your father was dead? You told me he was traveling but really he was dead?"

"Yes."

Miller wanted to be blown away by the strangeness of it, the insanity of lying about the very body of one's father—Living? Dead? Heaven? Perdition?—but instead he was overcome with the need to grab this woman, keep her, never again let her out of his sight.

He was out of cigarettes. He could smell, though, the nicotine on Blair's sweater, and he was glad she hadn't managed to quit. At least he'd left her with something. She had a huge tote bag slung over her arm, dwarfing her. He looked at the scar lining her chin, and wanted to punch it.

But instead he said, "You lied to everyone about your father. That he was always somewhere else."

"That's how I like to imagine it." Blair had one hand on the door frame now, as if for support. She pressed her lips together.

"Well," Miller said, "that's pretty fucking weird."

"Look, I wanted to give you this. Your father liked them, and I really have nothing else to do with them." She took a binder out of the tote bag, and Miller knew what it was.

"You don't have to," he said.

"I know." Then, at an obvious loss for anything else she added, "I'm just—well, I'm really sorry about your father."

"Yes," Miller said. "I'm sorry about yours."

• • •

He could have watched her walk down the hall, but at that moment he could not bear to see her disappear. He touched her hand for a second, mostly to nudge it off the door frame. Then he closed the door. For a moment he was dazzled by the ludicrousness of it all, but also by the smallest lusty thrill of seeing Blair again at his door, her strong legs, her delicate hands, the scar on her chin that he used to love to lick. She had been there at his door, she had been there for him, to say that she was sorry, to say that she knew how it felt, to say that her father was never an obstacle in the first place, to say that he was dead, like Stan was dead, that they were orphans together.

Miller leaned against a wall. Blair's father was dead.

Which meant that he was never an obstacle in the first place.

Which meant that the obstacles had lain elsewhere, in Blair's head, and in her heart.

Miller went into the bedroom and kicked one of his boxes over and over again. Blair's father was dead. Stanley was dead.

He lay down on the futon, and took a deep breath, and then he cried. He let himself cry, let the tears rip him open. He cried longer than he had since he was a child, and perhaps as long as he had ever cried at all. His throat ached. His nose ran.

But finally he stopped, and after he had stopped, he did what his father would have done.

He wiped his hands on his jeans, opened up Blair's binder, and began to examine her father's wonderful cards.

PART FOUR

(Primarily Concerning a Baby)

Tab A

Miller looks at the clock that hangs beside the bathroom wall. It is now 12:51, and Lisa's urine has been sitting on the counter in the bathroom for quite a while. Miller wonders if urine can grow stale and lose its powers of prophecy.

He lights a cigarette and bounces one of Harry's rubber balls off the bathroom door. Harry, asleep in the living room, snores and rolls over. "Hey, Lisa, the results should be in," Miller says. "Let's see what's what."

The ball rebounds and trickles toward his lap. It is round and red, not at all unlike the rubber ball that landed on his stoop this morning, which belonged to a dark-haired little girl in a raincoat. A little girl who glared at him. Miller looks at the cigarette burning between his thumb and his index finger; it seems to him sweetly carcinogenic amid the glaring possibility of new life.

"Okay," Lisa calls from the bathroom. "I'm almost finished."

"Look, I don't want to push you," Miller says, "but it's just that I think we should know, so that we can . . ." He stops for a minute. "So that we can figure out what to do next."

"Sure." Lisa opens the bathroom door and appears in a cloud of steam, her hair wrapped in a white towel. She is leaning forward on her crutches and smiling. The steam emerging from the bathroom smells like peppermint. "I thought

I'd do a little facial," she says. "I mean, as long as I was in there."

Miller stubs out his cigarette and stands up. "Look, what if it's positive?"

"It won't be positive," Lisa says. The mist evaporates and she stops smiling.

"But what if it is?"

"If it is," she says, "then it is." Miller is aware that this is no kind of answer but knows, too, that this answer is indisputable. She closes the bathroom door again.

He picks up Harry's ball and takes it into the bedroom, sits down on the bed, dribbles the ball a few times before it skitters away.

In the bathroom, Lisa is conducting a chemistry experiment, sticking tab A into the cup of pee, swirling it, and then placing tab A into the thimble cup of solution B and waiting to see the results.

Miller watches the ball settle into the corner of the room. Then he bends and pulls a shoebox full of baseball cards from under his bed. The shoebox contains just a small part of his collection, for Miller now owns thousands of cards: the ones his father gave him, the ones his father kept for himself, and the cards that belonged to Reynold Carter, still encased in leather, probably worth a quarter million dollars or more. The cards are arranged in various boxes and folders under the bed. Any thief could take them if he just knew where to look.

The particular shoebox Miller now holds is full of the cards he neglected as a child. He flips through them, studies the insignias on the baseball caps, the glowering third basemen, and the serene outfielders. Some of the cards are still in their silver foil. Some have slivers of petrified chewing gum stuck inside them.

The players have such beautiful names. Rusty and Carlos and Darryl and Angel. Barry and Francisco and Coot.

He's thinking: *I wonder if my son would be good at baseball.*

He's thinking: *What would Lisa say to naming our son Francisco or Coot?*

Coot Stanislaw Miller. Coot son-of-Lisa son-of-Joel. Coot Stanley. Coot Francisco.

Oh, please. Coot, no way.

Miller lights up again and then plucks a card at random from the box: Charlie Moore, a mediocre player, the third baseman on the Brewers from 1973 to 1986, batted .260, played in one World Series, which the Brewers lost. Nevertheless, Miller studies Moore's stats for several moments before realizing that there is no lesson to be learned from this man. He has given the world little, and ended up in a shoebox.

Then a spark from his cigarette jumps, as if of its own volition, onto the left corner of his card, and burns a neat little hole in it before disappearing. Is there a lesson here, then?

Miller opens the window. He's out of cigarettes now, which is just as well, because if nothing else the lesson may be that clearly he's a bit of a fire hazard. And anyway, if he's going to be a father, he should probably start smoking less.

Lisa will never let him smoke around the baby.

Lisa

Fifteen months ago, she had appeared like a vision at a crowded Krispy Kreme outpost on Fourteenth Street, holding a bag of glazed regulars and looking ashamed. "I don't usually do this," she said, to no one in particular. "Eat this many in a row." Lisa was wearing—he'll never forget it—nylon running pants and a Barnard sweatshirt that had been torn off at the collar. Torn at the collar: a Blair Carter trademark. Miller couldn't help but look longingly at her neck.

She smiled at him when she noticed he was watching her, and quickly straightened her ponytail with her free left hand. Miller was still on line to buy two or three chocolate glazed—it was already eight weeks since Blair had left, but still, all he could manage to swallow down were chocolate donuts and Starbucks mochas and Jack Daniel's. Twice Grant had come over and ordered Chinese for them both, under the theory that they needed to keep up their respective strengths for whatever tragedy might next befall them. But Miller had just poked glumly at his General Tso's and thought about sheikh babani with Blair, or greasy chop suey with his father. He'd had no appetite.

"Want a donut?" Lisa said, now holding the bag open to him. "Then you won't have to wait on line." Later, she confessed to him that this was the bravest thing she'd ever said to a stranger.

"What kind you got?" Miller asked.

"Glazed." She seemed to have large breasts.

"Sure," Miller said. He followed her outside, where they sat down on a splintery wooden bench and shared a donut in the January cold. He had been on Fourteenth Street because he'd walked there, aimlessly. Walking was one of the few activities he felt capable of these days. She was there because she liked to run at Chelsea Piers. The donuts, she said, were a comfort during a particular time of the month, and a reward for a lengthy run.

They finished the donuts and went for a Jack Daniel's at a bar across the street, and then they took a cab to her house in Park Slope. Miller was quiet, but Lisa was chatty enough for them both. A grade-school teacher, she said, first grade; she loved it, it was inspiring work. Children were good and innocent and smarter than you'd think. Children were the future.

She fell asleep within minutes after they'd finished a tepid round of lovemaking; the booze and the run and the sex knocked her out. It was three A.M. on a Saturday morning, and Miller still felt numb. A spent condom lay on the sheet next to him.

He felt around with his feet for his boxers at the bottom of the bed.

Then Lisa, sleeping, took hold of his pinky in her soft warm fist. She made a snuffling, snoring sound, and pushed her body against his, naked but for the Barnard sweatshirt. He felt the length of her, and the brush of her pubic hair against his thigh, and somewhere inside him something stirred, prompted by the way she was holding on.

He knew, at that very moment, that he could have this woman as long as he wanted her. He knew she'd never leave him. Fifteen months later, about this, he remained sure.

Romantic Comedy

The next weekend, lonely and drunk, with no better reading material than a bedraggled copy of the *New Yorker,* Miller left a message on Lisa's machine. She called back within minutes. They made plans to meet for dinner at a place she suggested; it turned out to be a proper sort of restaurant, with cloth napkins and leather-bound menus, and this evening set a pattern. Dinner at such restaurants, the check fifty-fifty, and afterward a rented romantic comedy back home at her apartment. Half the time Lisa would fall asleep on the couch, pinning his arm behind her back. He'd creep out at dawn, getting back to his place in time for Harry's morning walk. Other than setting the alarm and splitting the cost of dinner, Miller let Lisa take charge of their evenings out. She liked to hold his hand while they walked.

"Can I meet your friends?" she asked him, two months and seven dates in.

"I don't have too many friends," he said. They were standing in the Blockbuster in Park Slope, near the Woody Allens.

"What about Grant?"

"Grant's been working a lot these days."

"Oh." She picked up *Small Time Crooks* and fingered the side of the box. "Well, what about your friends from work?"

"I don't have too many friends from work, to be honest."

"I'd let you meet my friends," she said, placing the crooks back on the shelf. "Anytime you wanted. I was thinking we could make plans with my friend, Bonnie, and her husband; you'd like them."

"Why would I like them?"

"Why won't you let me meet your friends?" she asked quietly. He knew he was hurting her feelings, but he wasn't about to make promises to her that he didn't feel like keeping.

"I'm telling you," he said. "There's nobody for you to meet."

"Do you think they won't like me?"

"Who's they?" Miller said. "Which friends are you talking about? I have no friends! My girlfriend dumped me, my best friend's a recluse, my mother lives in California, my father's dead! I have no friends!" He ended his brief soliloquy shouting.

Lisa licked her lips and stormed out of Blockbuster.

Ah, fuck. Miller slid over to drama, then horror, and then out of the store, to find her shivering under the Blockbuster awning. It wasn't that cold out.

"What's wrong with you?"

"Your girlfriend dumped you months ago, Miller. She's your *ex*-girlfriend. *Your ex*. Although clearly you don't think I'm your girlfriend yet, and I must say I find that pretty damn disappointing, considering we've been going out for two months now."

Miller had neither the patience nor the inclination to fight with her. She was right, anyway—Blair *was* his ex-girlfriend, and if Lisa was not his current girlfriend, then he shouldn't be wasting all his money eating with her in fancy restaurants.

"I'm sorry," he said, because it was easy.

Lisa glared at him. It crossed his mind that she looked cute when she was annoyed.

"I've been through a lot," he said, lighting a cigarette.

"I know," she said. "I don't mean to be insensitive." She pulled the neck of her turtleneck up to her lips. "I just felt hurt, and I wanted to get it out of my system." She took his hand. "That way, my hurt won't come back to haunt us later. I won't turn passive-aggressive."

"I see," Miller said.

She lifted his hand to her mouth and kissed it. "It's really important to get rid of hurt while you're feeling it," she said. "It may sound dumb, but it's true."

"It's not dumb." He withdrew his hand.

"You finish that cigarette," she said, a relieved note in her voice. "I'll go pick out a movie."

Back in her apartment, they watched *Mighty Aphrodite*, and from the way she kissed his shoulder and his neck, Miller could tell that she was happy with the night's achievement. They had made it through their first fight. In the morning, she could tell her friends.

Recovery

"I need you to recommend a book to me," Bay said, on the phone from California. "Something that'll impress people. I want to sound like a smart cookie, like you."

"Who do you want to impress?"

Bay paused. "I have a date, okay? I met this fellow at the office; he came in, he flirted with me. So now I have a date. Is that all right with you?"

"Easy there, mom," Miller said. "That's great. Don't get defensive."

"Who's defensive?" Bay asked. "I've got a date. A real gentleman. He's in sprinklers." He could hear her blow a bubble in her gum and pop it. "Fire sprinklers, specifically. He has a business installing sprinklers in people's homes. Excellent money. You'd be surprised."

"That sounds terrific, mom."

"Don't be patronizing."

"Mom, really," Miller said. "It sounds terrific."

"And you?"

"I don't know, not much to report," Miller said. He rubbed Harry's stomach with his foot; Harry drooled and kicked his legs with pleasure. It was March, and the radiator was gurgling with steam heat. "I've sort of been seeing someone, I guess. She's a teacher."

"A teacher!" Bay said. "I always thought teaching was a very fine profession."

"First grade," Miller said. "Or second grade. I forget."

"Well, either way, it's a wonderful thing to be a teacher. First grade or second grade. Is she a nice girl? Can I meet her when I visit?"

"We'll see, mom." Bay was planning a return trip in a few months, to check on her son, make sure he was holding up all right. He thought maybe he would take her to a Mets game.

"It would be lovely to meet this teacher of yours. That's all I'm saying. I've got a date, you've got a date, this is wonderful news. Everybody's moving on."

A Good Girl

Well, not everybody.

Grant had waited, but Rachel did not return. So since the life of the heart had proved treacherous, he decided to devote himself to the life of the wallet. He left for work as the sun was rising and came home long after it had set. There were no more parties, no more women to distract him from the earning and accruing of money. Rumor had it that Rachel had taken up with an actor on some TV series, so Grant threw out his television. He didn't have time to watch it, anyway.

Miller went to visit him at his office one Sunday afternoon. "You look like shit," he said.

"You're one to talk," Grant rejoined. He was hunched over his desk, unshaven, a congealing slice of pizza resting on top of a pile of papers. He was wearing glasses, which Miller had never seen him wear before. His office smelled like dead plants and intestinal gas.

"You should throw out that cactus," Miller said.

Grant glanced over at the cactus on the windowsill and wiped his nose. "I thought I saw her getting out of a cab yesterday," he said. "And then I realized it was some dude. A tall skinny black dude. I'm losing my mind."

Miller took two warmish beers out of his knapsack and handed one to his friend.

"Then the other night, I thought—" Grant rested the beer against his cheek and looked up at the ceiling. "I was leaving here at three in the morning, right—it was a Friday night, and I was alone. I thought to myself, I should just get a girl."

"A girl?"

"A girl, you know. Just go to the phone book, look up a call girl or whatever, she could even meet me here, it wouldn't matter. Max in the next office does it all the time, and he's got a wife and kids in Westchester."

Grant looked like a figure out of Theodore Dreiser, the archetypically ruined man. Miller's heart felt a kick of sympathy, and he realized that it had been a long time since he'd been able to feel sorry for someone else.

"But I have never in my life paid for sex," Grant said. His shoulders drooped.

"You wouldn't have to pay if you didn't want to," Miller said. "You could just go to a bar or something. Pick someone up. It'd lift your spirits."

"Don't condescend, motherfucker," Grant said. He cracked open his beer and lifted an eyebrow. "Well, it seems to have worked for you, anyway."

Miller shrugged. "She was buying donuts."

"Donuts, sure," Grant said. "It's good to have a woman who eats donuts." He took a sip of beer. "Anyway, I like her. None of that flashy bullshit."

"How do you know you like her? You met her for half an hour." Miller, moved less by Lisa's histrionics than by Grant's curiosity, had introduced them over coffee the previous weekend. It had gone smoothly, and afterward, Lisa confided that she thought Grant was cute.

"I can just tell with women," Grant said. "Trust me. She's a good girl." He took off his glasses and rubbed his eyes, and when he put down his fists his eyes caught the light and sparkled. "Listen, I'll tell you about that kind of girl," he said. "Down-to-earth, kind of a homebody, right—but she's got this kind of attitude, this balls-out, I'm-in-charge-here kind of thing. Like she's not going to let you get away with shit. But she'll take care of the house and make dinner and stuff, and you're never going to have to worry that she's going to turn you into a fucking cuckold."

"She wants me to move into her place. She says my apartment feels too creepy."

"Your apartment's a goddamn ghost town," Grant said. "Get the hell out of there. You never even managed to unpack."

"I have a system. With my boxes. I know where everything is."

"Homeless people live in boxes," Grant said. "You're not homeless. You have no excuse."

• • •

Back on the Upper East Side, Miller took an inventory of his boxes. He slit one open with his key. It was full of books: *Rabbit, Run; The Bonfire of the Vanities; Your Neutered Pet and You.*

He looked over at Harry, snoring in the sunniest corner of the room, and he thought about the dog's salvation. What would the dwarf Barbara think if she knew he was moving the dog for the second time in a year? According to ASPCA literature, it wasn't such a good idea to move a dog around too frequently. Dogs got attached to places just like their owners. Places, and people too.

Miller scratched Harry behind the ears. "Do you miss her, Harry?" The dog woke up and raised one eyebrow at Miller. "I bet you do." Harry's paws were large and gentle. He rested his head on them and eyed Miller with what seemed a philosophical expression. Miller held his breath, momentarily captivated by the idiot hope that his dog might answer him.

"So what is it, Harry? What have you got for me?"

Harry sneezed. Then he closed his brown eyes, rolled over, and fell right back asleep.

Cohabitation

Moving in with Lisa was easy; all of Miller's stuff was already packed. He rented another U-Haul, this time with SEE ALBANY! painted on the side, and took his things back across the Triborough Bridge, onto the Brooklyn-Queens Expressway, and across Fourth Avenue into Park Slope. Harry sat between them on the front seat, Lisa drove, and Miller smoked.

"This is going to be so great," she said, holding tight to the steering wheel. Her voice wavered. Bay's brief visit had left an anxious aftertaste.

"It will," Miller said, tossing his cigarette butt out the window. Lisa had not spoken again of his suggestion, during Bay's visit, that they "not do this," but it remained palpable in the optimism with which she discussed the move. ("We're going to have so much fun! We can cook dinner together every night!") On his end, Miller prepared for the move with cool perseverance. On the way home from work he picked up frothy drinks from Starbucks and walked around his neighborhood. He wouldn't miss it.

When moving day came, Miller didn't take all that much with him: clothing (Debra's T-shirts, Grant's sweaters, a few pairs of shoes), books, his shoeboxes filled with his father's baseball cards, and Blair's. After a bit of cajoling—Lisa already had a sofa bed for guests—Miller threw out his old futon. It was ratty, anyway, with a stain on the yellowed ticking and a rip slowly extending along the seam. Further, there was no room for it in Lisa's three rooms in Park Slope, and as she pointed out it really was quite possible that the thing had fleas.

Miller dragged the futon down four flights of stairs, thumping and bumping along the banister. Fifteen minutes after he'd left it on the curb someone came along and scavenged it, took it to a new bedroom or street corner somewhere in New York City. But before Miller had dragged it down, he'd examined it with the focus of a scientist in search of an atom. He scanned it from side to side, top to bottom, even feeling in the recesses of the seams until he finally found what he wanted: three inches long, a fine gold-blond hair.

• • •

They parked the U-Haul in front of Lisa's building on Fourteenth Street, a brownstone with a stoop. It was a cool summer Thursday and her neighbors were all at work. Harry bounded out and immediately peed on the boxed magnolia on the sidewalk. "See?" Lisa said. "He feels right at home." She presented her cheek to the dog, who licked her with enthusiasm; Harry, Miller thought, you're such a slut.

The Park Slope apartment had been cleaned and ruthlessly

organized—the books were alphabetized, of course, but now, too, were the spices in the spice rack and the medicines in the vanity. Lisa had emptied out four drawers for him on the bottom of her dresser, and she'd bought a round cushy mat for Harry to sleep on. She'd stocked the kitchen with things she knew Miller liked: beer, Cheez-Its, curry powder. Miller brought in his first batch of belongings, a duffel bag of underwear, and was hit by the smell of Pine-Sol. Lisa had scrubbed for him. Gotten down on her knees.

"Thanks for doing all this," Miller said. She was right behind him, carrying a box of his CDs. He dropped his duffel on the sofa. She had bought him a new bookshelf and squeezed it in next to her own.

"Well, of course." Lisa's long hair was tied back in a sweaty ponytail. "I want you to feel at home."

"I already do," Miller said. He made a show of sitting down on the couch, leaning back on the cushions, crossing his legs on the coffee table. "Look at me," he said. "Right at home already. It's like I've lived here all my life." He pulled Lisa to him and kissed her on the cheek.

"Oh, good," she said. "I'm so glad you like it. I was worried—"

"Nothing to worry about," Miller interrupted. He paused, and then added, "Nothing at all"—as if by saying it twice he could make it true.

Motherhood

And now it's 12:59. The digital numbers on the alarm clock next to the bed have silently moved forward. Watching the windows in the room grow brighter as the sun comes out, Miller begins to sweat. In the bathroom, Lisa is singing "Midnight Train to Georgia."

Oh, lovely Lisa.

She'd be such a wonderful mother.

Miller rolls over onto his stomach, fiddles with the stitching on the handmade quilt.

She'd carry a baby well, with her strong legs and stomach muscles. And as her belly grew, she would wear flowing shirts and long skirts, and use her pregnancy to explain to her first-grade students the miracle of life. She would accept strangers' congratulations, but gamely rebuff the offer of a seat on a crowded subway, choosing to hold the pole just like she did before she became pregnant. She'd never want her pregnancy to seem like an infirmity.

Her labor would be easy, because she was in good shape and had wide-ish hips.

Miller knew that Lisa would mother a baby who'd grow up to be confident and determined. A girl who would believe in things like hard work and empowerment, or a boy who was generous and well-liked by women. A smart child, well-behaved, and even if that child turned out to be unpopular in junior high, he would still greet the future with the confidence ensured by his superior upbringing. He would not care what the philistines in junior high said about him. He would know his own strength. He would grow up to be a chemist or a social worker.

Or their daughter, who would make multicultural paper dolls and grow her hair long and wild, and stick flowers in it.

Or maybe this child, son or daughter, would turn out to be more than the sum of his or her parents, and would improve upon the hand that he or she had been dealt. This outstanding child would cure cancer, or write a famous poem, or place in an Olympic slalom event.

Miller thinks: *But I myself have never placed in an Olympic slalom event.*

Miller thinks: *And I myself have never written a famous poem.*

He imagines this child, but there are holes in what he can imagine. He cannot see himself working on grade-school homework projects; he cannot see building this kid a secret hide-away in the backyard; he cannot see taking this child to base-ball games or giving him boxes of baseball cards. And it occurs to him that this lack of imagination is due to the fact that he cannot see himself loving Lisa the way a father should love the mother of his children.

Miller thinks: *I should love her like my father once loved my mother.*

Miller thinks: *I should love her the way that I could have loved Blair, if she had let me.*

Miller thinks: *I do not love Lisa in the right way, and I do not love her enough.*

Miller thinks: *Then we should not have this baby.*

Reproduction Is the Flaw of Love

Lying on the bed, shirtless, sweating, Miller waits for Lisa to come tell him the news.

Harry snuffles over and looks up at the bed mournfully, as though he wished he could prop himself upon it and lie down next to his master. The dog's weight works against him, how-ever, so instead he just plops down at the foot of the bed and gazes up at Miller with fondness. He balances his head on his paws.

The sun is shining brightly now, and the room is noticeably hotter; it's turning into a beautiful day. Harry sticks out his tongue, and Miller closes his eyes. When Lisa enters the room, banging the door with her crutches, he is startled awake.

"Miller," she says. She is sitting on the bed next to him, touching his shoulder. In the bright sunlight, Lisa is more beautiful than he's ever given her credit for.

"Listen," she says, "I'm not pregnant."

"What?"

"I'm not pregnant," she says again. "The test was negative."

She's smiling, but Miller senses she feels the tiniest remorse. Her eyes don't meet his. "So we've got nothing to worry about," she says.

"Oh," Miller says. He waits to feel something. "I guess that's good," he says.

"Sure," Lisa says. "It's good." She lies back on the bed, her cast dragging on the floor. Traces of red lipstick have seeped into the cracks of her lips and bled into the skin around her mouth. Her long hair fans out behind her on the bedspread. The ratty pink bathrobe falls open, and he can see the pale space between her breasts.

In their bedroom is a dresser with photographs, framed shots of the two of them, another of Harry, and one of Grant and Miller five years ago, drunk, each holding a bottle of Goldschlager above the other's head. There is a picture of Lisa and her parents, and the picture of Miller's father being fed by his mother. There are piles of books, and under the bed, a collection of cards.

"I guess I should call Bonnie, see what time we should go." Lisa reaches for her crutches, struggles to stand up.

"Sure," Miller says, and touches her cast.

The walls are painted a nice yellow color, perhaps not far from the saffron Rachel had once suggested for his apartment on the Upper East Side. Miller's still not exactly sure what saffron walls look like.

Lisa had offered him an escape from that misguided apartment. She had offered him someone to come home to, someone who would cook him wholesome dinners and ask how his day was. She is nice to his dog, and he had known from the day he met her that she would never leave him. But that doesn't mean he has to stay.

"So you're sure, then?" he asks. "The test was negative?"

"One hundred percent," Lisa says. "In fact, I think I'm starting to get crampy. Like I might get my period any second. Isn't that a laugh?" she says, not smiling.

"It's a riot," Miller says, and closes his eyes again. They have photographs, and a nice apartment, and a dog, and a friendship. But Lisa isn't pregnant. There will be no baby.

And so Miller can't help but wonder, among everything they have, exactly what it is that they have left.

EPILOGUE

(Primarily Concerning Miller, Six Months Later)

Twelfth Street

It is his first apartment with a dishwasher, and Miller can't help himself. He washes everything. Coffee spoons, doggie bowls, wineglasses, ashtrays. He tries to wash an old blue baseball cap but the thing comes out misshapen and greenish; he tries again with Jockey shorts and they exit the dishwasher steamy and in fine condition. "What do you think, Harry? Not too shabby, right?"

The apartment, like so many of Miller's favorite things, came courtesy of Grant, whose new girlfriend owns two buildings in the West Village. Heather, the girlfriend, is tall and blond and uncommonly generous; she offered Miller a quarter off the rent if he'd agree to walk her dog on the mornings she wants to sleep late at Grant's house. "Take it," Grant said. "Park Slope is killing you." So Miller did, and the deal works out nicely for everyone: Miller can afford this luxurious apartment, Grant and Heather can stay in on Sundays, and Harry has a new friend, a flirtatious Shih Tzu named Lola who lives on the eleventh floor.

Sometimes Miller takes the dogs up to the building's roof deck, about twenty square feet of fenced-in plywood with a view of the Hudson and New Jersey beyond. Harry, in particular, loves it on the roof; he struggles up the stairs with gritty fortitude, then plops down in the middle of the deck for a nap in the sun. Lola prefers to sit on Miller's lap and lick his face.

"A real roof deck?" Bay says, on the phone from San Francisco. She too has moved up in the world, living now in a Pacific Heights condo with her fire-sprinkler-magnate fiancé. "With a view and everything?"

"I'm up there right now," Miller says. It is the tail end of a Sunday afternoon in October; Miller is talking on his cell phone and scratching Harry's shoulders. Lola is fast asleep on his other side. "You'll see it when you come visit."

"And there's closet space?" asks Bay, who has heard enough about the vagaries of New York apartment living.

"A big one in the bedroom and a small one in the hall."

"Elevator?"

"Yep. I live on the seventh floor, remember?"

"Right, right, you told me."

Miller rubs at the sweet spot between Harry's ears, and the dog sighs with pleasure. "There's even an icemaker," he says. "In the fridge. So I don't have to bother with ice trays or anything—I can just press a button and the ice shoots into a bin in the freezer."

"Well, what can I say, honey?" Bay laughs. "Sounds like a palace. Sounds like the high life. And you have enough money?"

"I have enough money."

"And you're not lonely all by yourself?"

"I'm not lonely, mom," Miller says, which is true. In fact, he is less lonely now than he had been during the months right after the pregnancy test, when Miller and Lisa found themselves awkward, with little to say to each other. Lisa baked endless banana breads. Miller took Harry for long walks. Lisa went to the doctor to have her cast removed. Miller read *The Rise and Fall of the Third Reich.* When Heather offered Miller the discounted apartment, he asked Lisa what she thought of the idea. "Of course you should take it," she said. "This is becoming exhausting." Her voice was mild, but it was clear from the circles under her eyes that she could no longer try to make something from what had become, essentially, nothing. So Lisa went to visit her parents for a long weekend while Miller packed up his things; when she returned from Chicago, he and Harry had already begun to establish themselves on Twelfth Street.

"And so I guess you're happy, then," Bay says. "Let me tell you something, honey, that's a relief."

"Yes," he says. "It is."

After he hangs up the phone, Miller looks out at the view: a V-formation of Canada geese fly above the river, and on the piers, people stroll and jog. Miller smokes his last cigarette and watches them all; it makes him happy to see his fellow New Yorkers taking advantage of the last of autumn's warm days. Then, after the sun dips behind the horizon, and the city begins to grow dark, Miller tugs on Harry's and Lola's leashes, and he and the dogs head back inside.

Acknowledgments

Thanks to Elliot Grodstein, for teaching me what I needed to know about how a guy's mind works, and to Jessie and Iain Kennedy for cheering me on when I needed the most cheering. Many thanks also to my dad for teaching me to love baseball, my mother for urging me to keep writing, and my grandparents for their endless dedication and support. My early readers, Binnie Kirshenbaum, Aaron Hamburger, Gordon Haber, and Kelly Braffet, have my deepest gratitude, as does Ben Freeman, who makes every day happy. Seth Unger and Allison Jaffin remain the best freelance publicists money can't buy. Enormous thanks to Lutz Wolf for the deadline; Kate Elton for her incredible enthusiasm; and Margo Lipschultz for her cheerfulness, efficiency, and astounding knowledge of both the important and the truly bizarre. Finally, a very special thank-you to Susan Kamil and Julie Barer, the smartest, funniest, most fabulous women a writer could hope to have on her team.